WARDED BOND

NIGHTWOOD CLAN SERIES, BOOK 7

HARPER DAKOTA

Cover Design by: Jay Aheer

Editing by: Lori Parks

Warning:

This book contains mature themes and is intended to be read by ages 18+. Contains sex, some curse words, paranormal and magical themes, fated mates, and two men in a committed/loving relationship. Mentions of death of parents, kidnapping.

Trademark Acknowledgements:

The author acknowledges the following trademarks and trademark status of these items mentioned in the book, including: Keurig, Epsom Salt, Post-It.

To my family. I love you all.

To my readers. Thank you for going on this journey with me and for sticking through for all of the Nightwood Clan books!

To all the people who help me along the way with amazing covers, beta reading, proofreading, and formatting. Thank you for helping me make my books the best they can be.

WARDED BOND

Gage is used to being alone. He has his brother, although they don't see each other often. From the time they were born, their mother instilled in them the need to hide Gage's shifter side. To this day, they still hide their relationship from others. This past year has changed everything though and Gage is adjusting to having a family and friends in the Nightwood Clan. What he never expected was for his mate to show up and his brother to go missing.

Elliot has always felt like an oddball. Of course, that could be because he was the only human in a family of vampires. They adopted him when his living conditions were less than ideal, and he's always been grateful, but that also meant that they were always overprotective. Finally, he gets a chance at freedom when the seer of the family sends him on his way. He doesn't think he'll actually lose all the bodyguards, but one can hope.

Can Gage and Elliot find the time to solidify their bond amid the outside chaos? Or will someone else try to destroy it for their own gain?

PRE-NOTE FROM THE AUTHOR

Thank you for choosing my book to read! I hope you enjoy it.

If this is your first time reading one of my books, or it has been a while in between reads, here are some helpful things so you don't feel lost.

There is a character list in the back of the book.

Mates and members of the Clan can speak telepathically to each other. This type of communication is indicated with a single apostrophe and the words are in italic.
Example: *'I can't wait to see you,'* Gage said.

Gage and his animal side are more of a separate entity than normal shifters. They can communicate to each other telepathically as well. This is indicated by words in italics, no apostrophes.
Example:
Stop trying to take over, Gage told his griffin.
Mine, his animal side stated smugly.

Text messages are indicated with a name in capital letters and are in bold with a colon.

Example:

ELLIOT: I'll be there soon.

GAGE: Drive safely.

Nightwood Clan members and their respective mates:

Rolf (Rolfston) - Shaye

Sam - Tess

Doc (Albert) – Emma

Ian - Berkley

Gawain - Merri (Meredith)

Duncan - Marge

Gage - Elliot

PROLOGUE
ELLIOT

"It's time."

Elliot looked up from what he was working on, hands dusted with flour and bits of cookie dough. He had been rolling out cookies when his aunt came in the kitchen and made the random statement. He searched his memory, trying to think of anything he had on the calendar. As far as he knew, the only thing he had was this order that he needed to ship out tomorrow.

"Time for what?"

"You to leave, spread your wings, find your own path, fulfill your destiny, find your place…how many more phrases do I need to use?" his aunt asked.

"Since when was I allowed to leave?" Elliot asked, a bit of sarcasm in his voice.

"It's not like you're a prisoner," his mother jumped in, indignant, coming to stand beside his aunt. "I just want you close so we can protect you. You're fragile."

"I'm human," he pointed out. "Not the same thing."

"You're more fragile than us," she rebutted. "You're so breakable. That's why there's always someone with you or watching over you," she added sadly.

"You could always turn me, then I wouldn't be so break-able," he pointed out. It was an old argument, one he never won. For as much as they worried, you would think they would want him stronger, but they never agreed to turn him.

"That's not for us to do," his aunt replied.

"That doesn't make sense," he said angrily.

"The visions were clear. You're ours, and ours to protect but we weren't to turn you. Our job was to protect you until it was time for you to leave. You're going to find a place to call your own. There you'll find what you're looking for and what you want to be."

"Thanks, that's clear as mud. Where am I supposed to be going? Do I just wander around hoping it jumps out at me?" Elliot asked, just a little bit heavy on the sarcasm. He knew he sounded a bit of a brat, but dealing with his aunt's visions and her cryptic messages was frustrating at times. It was rare that he got a straightforward answer, and this was the last thing he expected today.

"Nope. You're going to Rockfort, Tennessee to see your wonderful friend Shaye. She's such a nice girl. Word has it she's a vampire now. Her mate has created this unique Clan, a mix of all different types of paranormals. I've even heard a few rumors that the whole town is warded."

"Is that why you're letting me go there?" he asked. This whole thing was making his head spin. He had been always overprotected, his mother worried that he would get hurt. The fact that they were sending him off, supposedly on his own, was just bizarre at this point in his life.

"No. That's helpful to keep your mother calm," his aunt said with a pointed glance at his mother, "but this is where the visions have you going. You're supposed to be there. They're having some issues with hunters, which is why the town is warded. I can't see it clearly, but you're meant to help them. Just remember we're always your family, even if you get adopted into another one."

"I'm going to go get your packing started," his mother said, tears in her eyes as she left the room.

"Ma," Elliot started to call after her.

"Let her be. She's known this has been coming, she's just emotional about it," his aunt said, although her eyes were also a little shiny. "Now, this is what fate has shown for you, but remember this is always your home. No matter what. Go give your friend a call and I'll reserve you a room in town. I don't know how much room they have at the Clan home, so I'll get you a hotel room or something. You can always cancel it and stay with them if they offer."

Elliot watched as his aunt walked out of the room, looking down at her phone and wiping her eyes. He sighed, putting the cookies in the oven, and washing the sticky residue off his hands before he grabbed his phone. He wasn't really sure why it was so important that he go now. He wasn't a stranger to having things suddenly change because of one of his aunt's visions. When his mother had found him, abandoned near a dumpster, his aunt had been overcome with the strongest vision in her life, or so the story went. They worked through some not quite legal backdoor channels to adopt him into their family. He loved them all and they never really treated him differently. Except when it came to anything they viewed as his safety. A lot of their family lived here, although he didn't think they ever officially formed a Clan. Someone was always nearby.

He'd been sickly when they first found him, malnourished, dirty, and speech delayed. He was about two or three from their best guess, and they celebrated his birthday as the day they found him. His dad had hired an investigator, trying to find more about his history, but they hadn't uncovered anything. His parents had never been able to have children of their own, which was part of the reason he thought his mom hovered and worried so much.

"Hey, cuz. I hear you're getting sprung," his cousin Baz said, strolling into the kitchen.

"Apparently," Elliot replied.

"It's a good thing, right? You've always wanted to explore more," his cousin said, a question in his voice.

"Yeah, I guess."

"What's wrong?" Baz asked. He was the cousin Elliot was closest to and was great at picking up nuances in his voice.

"I don't know," Elliot replied, frustrated. "I guess now that it's here, I'm...not scared, but hesitant? Worried? Like why now, why me, what am I supposed to do? Is Shaye even really my friend, or did Mom and Dad and Auntie bring her here?"

"Wow. Okay. Let's unpack that. I get that you might be nervous, after all you've never gone somewhere on your own. You've always known at least someone from the family was nearby. If it helps at all, I really doubt your mom will let you travel all the way there without someone tailing you," Baz said with a smile.

Elliot had to laugh, but it was probably true.

"Now, I know that Shaye came because of a job offer; whether or not the parents were behind that I have no idea. I also know that they can't *make* you feel a connection and form a friendship with someone. Any friendship you made with her is genuine and between you two. Maybe it was a happy coincidence, and you would have had to go to Rockfort anyway, even if you had never met her.

"I have no idea what you're supposed to do. I don't know that even Mom knows, despite all the visions she's had. Don't put pressure on yourself; remember, not all things that make a difference are huge. You probably won't be leading a charge into battle, but maybe it's a connection you form with some-one, maybe it's a friendship, maybe it's a relationship, maybe you finally get your own bakery and your amazing cookies change someone's life," Baz added with a smile.

"I don't think that last one is real," Elliot said, a smile making its way onto his face.

"I'm going to have withdrawal," Baz pouted.

Elliot shook his head at his best friend and cousin. "Maybe I can overnight ship you cookies, or you can come to visit," he pointed out.

"I will once you get settled," Baz promised. "Call if you need anything and I'll gather the cousins and come right away."

Elliot nodded, stepping up to his cousin to be wrapped in a hug.

PROLOGUE

GAGE

G age looked down at the squirming little bundle in his mother's arms. "What is that?" he asked, sniffing the air.

"This is your little brother," she said with a smile.

"He doesn't smell like me," Gage said, looking at the tiny boy.

"No, he doesn't. I don't think anyone is going to smell quite like you, love. You're unique."

"Is he going to like me?" Gage asked. He was eager to have someone to play with. His mother kept them separate from other paranormals and he got bored only having her to play with, especially when she was too busy.

"I think you're going to be the best of friends," she said.

Gage remembered hoping that would be true. Years later, his mother was killed by hunters and he and his brother fled their home, hiding in the woods, hunting and foraging their food. Gage had been terrified that his brother Marco would be killed like his mother and had been focused on finding a way to stop that from happening, keeping them on the move and as separated from people as possible.

However, Marco was still a growing boy and had been

growing through all his clothes. Gage hadn't wanted to steal things, but he needed to provide for his brother, so he worked a few odd jobs or traded work for goods. Technically Gage was considered an adult and could find a few jobs as they travelled. They usually moved on quickly, but this last stop had been longer. Something had drawn him here and one night he discovered why.

The magic drew him to an old abandoned church. As he explored the area, he found an old parchment locked away in stone. He could smell the magic coming from it and he worked over several nights to work it loose. It spoke of rare paranormals and Gage had been so relieved to realize that while he may be the only griffin, he wasn't the only weird one. As he had continued reading, he began sobbing when he realized that it was telling him he was immortal. He didn't want to lose his brother and be left alone in this world. When he calmed down, he forced himself to keep reading. Oh! Gage had raced back to their camp, finding Marco roasting a rabbit.

Gage grabbed a cup, cutting his arm.

"Stop! What are you doing?" Marco said, trying to grab the knife from him.

"I'm saving you," Gage said, showing Marco the parchment.

"Do you think it's true?"

"I hope so. Do you want to find out?" Gage asked.

Marco nodded and Gage continued with the ritual.

He watched as Marco drank his blood, sensing the change in his brother immediately. Most people couldn't feel the magic like he could, but he could sense other people's animals or what type of paranormal they were, if they had magic and what kind, he could even block some magic on himself. He studied his brother, almost seeing the spell course through his body, changing him. Gage had been so relieved. Now he wouldn't ever lose his brother.

1

Gage felt like bashing his head against the wall would be more productive than this stupid investigation. Barry was good at hiding his tracks, he would give him that. Of course, paper records were even harder to come by regarding Barry's father. Although a few of the breeding camps had been found, he knew there were probably more out there. They still hadn't been able to find the main location, the family estate where they believed he was holding other paranormals captive.

At least they had finally found enough evidence to convince the rest of the Convocation to take a look into Barry. Gawain's friend Rob had a contact inside of the Convocation who promised to keep them informed if something was found. Their governing body wasn't always known for sharing what they had, even on less scandalous cases. An arrest warrant had been issued for Barry and his two cronies, but so far Barry was in the wind. There was no trace of him and the places his accomplices knew about had turned up nothing.

Marco had been cleared of being involved. He'd found the first two camps, and there had been a few on the Convocation board that had raised concerns of him being involved. When his scent wasn't at any of the other camps they found, it was hard for them to keep arguing to keep Marco out of the investigations. Gage still wasn't sure what prompted them to question Marco. It was such an odd thing and didn't make any logical sense. He was beginning to wonder if there were more people involved than just Barry and his two cronies. At least now they had two people, Marco and Rob's contact, who could help keep them updated.

Even though they had been alone for so long, both he and Marco claimed this town as theirs. Even if Marco wasn't here much and actually lived someplace else. Rolf and his friends had been here long before he had arrived, but they'd made it a welcoming place. Gage was just so used to keeping himself apart, that it had taken him almost twenty years to lower his walls enough to feel like he was becoming friends with them. Of course, it could have to do with the new additions to the Clan as well. It was hard to resist when Emma's quiet mothering, Shaye's calming presence, and even Tess's dad jokes and puns created this wonderful inviting atmosphere.

Even his oldest friend Marge had been drawn in. He couldn't believe that she was mated and now a mother. That child was something else; his TruthSpeaker powers were like nothing Gage had experienced before. The fact that he could resist other TruthSpeakers and extend that protection to people besides himself was outstanding, and something that would make him valuable to anyone who knew about it. It was a good thing Barry hadn't known about that particular aspect of Jimmy's abilities or he more than likely would have placed a kill spell on the boy like he had with his assistant.

Gage leaned his head against the back of his chair. Sometimes he felt confined by his position of Warden and Sheriff. He would love nothing more than to join the Nightwood Clan and have that family feeling all the time, but it wasn't allowed as a Warden. They had never told anyone about the bond Gage and Marco shared, at least not until they recently had shared it with the Nightwoods. He knew he was in a better position to protect the people he and his beast now saw as theirs as a Warden, but part of him still longed to be part of their family. Of course, they had all welcomed him in and told him that he and Marco were part of the family, regardless of if they could take the pledge. But feeling that bond would have been nice.

He knew he was the only one in the building, as he was working late and the deputy on night shift was doing a drive through town and around the outskirts of the ward, making sure nothing was amiss. Letting loose control over his powers, Gage let them flow out, tired of keeping them contained. He allowed himself to feel the freedom for a minute or two before pulling them back inside, tamping them down so they wouldn't be felt by others. His power was incredibly strong and was a dead giveaway that he wasn't normal. His mother had taught him at an early age how to hide it. Marco also had learned how to hide his; although not as strong as Gage, he was still incredibly strong. As soon as he pulled it back in, his phone pinged.

ROLF: Shaye says you need to come over for dinner. We felt the surge. You okay?

GAGE: I'm good, just needed to release some steam.

He sent the message and then paused in typing. He really did want to go to dinner, but still felt like an imposition at times. It was nothing they did, it was all him, but tonight was one of those nights.

SHAYE: You're not an imposition. Now get over here for dinner. I made cookies for dessert and Tess made these amazing pretzel rolls for dinner, but I can't have any until everyone is here. :(

Gage had to laugh. Shaye's love of bread was well known, and he loved the food the family served.

GAGE: I'll be there. I have to close up a few things and let my deputy know I'm done for the night.

Gage closed his computer and sent a text off to his deputy letting him know he was locking the building. He had his own set of keys to get back in. As he climbed into his SUV, he made sure his powers were at his normal setting. He didn't want to upset Emma when he got there; she had gotten so much better, but sometimes things still startled her, and he never wanted to be a source of fear for her. She had dealt with too much in her life already.

'You get an invite to dinner too?' his brother asked him telepathically.

'Yup. You coming?' Gage asked.

Gage waited for a response, knowing it was even harder for his brother to integrate into the family, no matter how much he wanted to. Gage at least saw them more frequently since he was stationed in town.

'Are you?' Marco asked.

'I am. I need something positive right now. I know you've got to be frustrated too. You should come,' Gage encouraged.

'Okay. I'll finish up and be there in a few minutes,' Marco finally said.

'See you there,' Gage replied. Turning his car on, he pulled out and headed to the estate. Punching in the gate code, he pulled through the rounded driveway, parking on the far side with his car facing toward the street. He didn't think he would get called out, but wanted to be prepared to leave quickly if needed.

Ian answered the door, handing him a drink. "Ye best be prepared. They're going to ply ye wi' love and food," he warned with a smile.

"I'm okay with that," Gage replied. "Can I help in any way?"

Ian shook his head. "It's all done, just waiting on Marco."

Gage followed him farther into the house, seeing everyone

hanging out in the kitchen and living room. The dining table had been set and he drew a deep breath, drawing in all the wonderful scents coming from the kitchen.

Marco arrived a few minutes later and Gage could see his brother's shoulders drop as he was able to relax. Although Shaye gave them both some space, he could feel her pumping out the calming vibes. He knew she had some empathy to go with her healing gift, but he was still surprised she had felt that both he and Marco needed this.

It was quiet for the first few minutes as everyone got their dinner.

"Is your friend coming tomorrow?" Marge asked Shaye.

"Yup, afternoon time frame, I think," she replied. "I haven't seen him in a while, so I was going to invite him over for a late lunch or snack and maybe dinner, depending on how he feels."

Gage listened as he ate. He had secretly run a background check on Elliot and there was very little information available. He had been adopted when he was a toddler and Gage strongly suspected his parents were paranormals. There weren't any red flags though and if the wards let him through, he wouldn't be a danger to them.

2

E lliot reached the border of the ward. He had always been able to sense magic. It felt like a tingle or goose bumps. He waved out the window to whichever family member had been assigned to trail him here. Taking a deep breath, he drove through and let the GPS guide him to the hotel. He drove slowly down the main street, looking out the windows.

"Recalculating," the GPS informed him. It always sounded so disapproving when he got off route.

Elliot laughed, he was driving the entire main street on purpose and would turn around at the end to get back to the hotel. It was a cute-looking town with a nice-looking park, a bakery, some other shops, a large library, the hospital and a mechanic on one end, the clinic where Shaye worked more toward the middle of the town. It was nice. He thought he would enjoy being here.

He parked at the hotel, pulling out only one suitcase. He was going to leave the other one in the car in case he did end up staying at the Clan home; everything he needed was in the one bag anyway. The other one was full of extra clothes. If he moved here, like his cousin thought he would, he would need to go back home and get the rest of his things.

"Hello, are you checking in?" the woman behind the desk asked with a smile.

"Yes, for Elliot—"

"Ah! Gotcha right here. Here's your room key, if you need more towels just call down. We have donuts in the morning from the local bakery. They have all sorts of delicious things there. The Black Wolf Brewery offers lunch and dinner and brunch on the weekends. Here's a little town map with the stores listed," she added, handing him a pamphlet. "There's a Keurig over there, along with a few touristy type of books, if you're wanting coffee."

"Thank you," he said, taking the key and pamphlet from her hand.

He found his room easily and took a few minutes to look around. The bed was a queen, and it was the perfect firmness as he sat down to test it. Poking at the pillows, he was happy to discover they had a nice mix of firm and smooshy. He preferred a firmer pillow and hated the pillows that collapsed as soon as any weight were put on them. It was nice that the hotel offered both. Walking to the bathroom, it looked pretty standard, complete with little travel-sized bottles of lotion and soaps. Elliot opened the blinds fully, pleased with his view. He could see the green tree-covered mountains. There were a few lazy clouds drifting by. He wondered if he would be able to see the infamous fog that gave the mountains their name. He unpacked a few items and sent a text to Shaye, letting her know he had arrived.

SHAYE: Do you want to come over for lunch or do you want to settle in first? No pressure!

Elliot took a minute to think about it. He was a little tired after his drive, and he knew Shaye would be fine with whatever decision he made. She would never be one to push someone to hang out if they didn't want to. He didn't know if he wanted to go explore the town or check in with Shaye and see if he could figure out why he might have been sent here. It had been such a whirlwind since his aunt announced it was time for him to leave; he'd been packed and sent on his way the next day. Logically, he knew that his family wasn't trying to get rid of him, and that this was supposed to be what he was meant to do, but it still felt rushed and a little off-putting. His inner child wanted to stomp his feet and rebel against the thought that he didn't have as much control of his life as he wanted, which he knew was silly.

ELLIOT: Would you care if I explored the town first, maybe came over for dinner instead?

He figured the town would be friendly enough if Shaye had decided to stay here. With her gifts, she would have a hard time staying if the town was horrible, even with her mate here.

SHAYE: No, that's fine! I love the bookstore/café, the bakery is great, Sam's place is the Black Wolf Brewery (great burgers, fries, shakes), and the library is gorgeous. Sundays are game night after dinner, just to warn you what you're getting into tonight. Six o'clock for dinner?

ELLIOT: Sounds perfect!

He figured he'd stop by the bakery and grab something for dessert so he didn't show up empty-handed. Grabbing his keys and wallet, he headed out to explore the town. It was getting closer to autumn, but it was still warm, no signs of the leaves changing yet. Elliot quickly walked through the one end of town as he didn't need the office supply store, the mechanic, fire department, or hospital. He did make a note of the grocery store though in case he needed to make a food run. The farmer's market was a large open-sided wood structure. He thought it would be fun to explore when it was open.

As he passed the police station, his skin lit up. Holy crap that was a lot of magic in there. All of his arm hairs were standing up. He would have to ask Shaye what was up with that building, he thought as he hurried by. He slowed down as he came to the library. It was a gorgeous building; lots of stone, columns by the front doors, stained glass windows. Looking at his watch, he figured he had plenty of time to check out the town and see what the library offered. Pulling open the large wood door, he walked into the two-story building. The middle was open all the way to the ceiling, the back and sides having a U-shaped upper floor. The second floor had metal railings instead of solid walls, making it feel more open. There were wood bookcases, some of them ornately decorated. He would guess this was a pretty old library; it was gorgeous in a way that the newer ones lacked. There was also magic in this building.

Walking farther in, Elliot noticed the help desk sitting in the middle of the room.

"Welcome in. Can I help you find anything?" the woman asked as he stood there looking around.

"I'm just looking but thank you. I got into town today and my friend recommended the library," he said. He was still getting tingles of magic, but he couldn't tell if it was from her or from farther back in the library. Maybe it was both.

The woman looked at him and he swore he saw her lightly sniff the air.

"This is going to sound strange, but are you Elliot?"

He was startled. "Yes," he said a little hesitantly.

"I'm Marge," she said, holding out a hand to shake. "I'm part of Shaye's Cl—uh, cluster of friends here. We're kind of one big family. She's excited to see you again."

Elliot had a feeling she was going to say Clan, but knew he was human. He had a lot to explain to Shaye when he saw her. She must have told everyone to keep the paranormal stuff quiet. He also suspected that Marge was checking him out; not in a sexual way, but in a protective of her friend way. He wondered why she would be cautious of him, other than him being human. But considering that Shaye had been human not that long ago, he didn't think it was a bias. His aunt did say they had some troubles here recently, so maybe that was it.

"I'm exploring the town right now, but coming over for dinner tonight. I was told it was game night?" he said questioningly. He wanted to be friendly with any of Shaye's new friends.

"Sundays are family dinner and game night. We all make a point of being there; the rest of the week gets crazy with everyone's schedules, but Sundays we all keep for family time. You're going to be dropped immediately into the deep end of our craziness, but they're all good people and it's a lot of fun."

"Ma! Can I go to Dave's house to play a new game he got?" a young boy ran up to the desk from the back.

"Can Duncan walk you over?" Marge asked him.

"Yeah. I already asked," the boy said, impatiently bouncing from foot to foot.

"Okay, but we're going to need to pick you up at five thirty to make it to Sunday dinner," Marge warned him.

"I know; Ian said he found a new game." The boy grinned.

"Have fun. Maybe we can have Dave over next weekend. I'll ask his mom," Marge told him, giving the boy a quick hug before he ran to the back of the library again.

"Sorry. Anyway, game night is a lot of fun. If there are any books you want to check out, I can get you a library card. We'll just use Rolf's address," she told him with a smile.

"Thanks, I'm just doing a quick tour today, but it looks like a great library. I'm definitely going to need to come back and explore it some more," Elliot said. He had a feeling there was even more to the library than just the great architecture. He couldn't wait to hear all about it from Shaye. He hadn't had many people outside of his family that he could talk to about paranormal stuff and he was looking forward to having more friends to talk to.

"Have fun, I look forward to getting to know you tonight," Marge said before moving to help another patron.

Elliot walked around the library, seeing a good selection of new releases and older books, some of which looked like antiques. There was a door in the back that screamed magic, and he guessed that was what he had sensed earlier. He waved to Marge as he made his way back to the front and walked back outside.

He was getting a little hungry but didn't want to be full for dinner, so he passed the brewery/restaurant, although the smells coming from it were tempting. He turned into the park, keeping to the main path. It was a neat area with grills and picnic areas, playgrounds, a fountain. It was good sized for a small town. As he worked his way closer to the entrance, the smell of baking sugar had him crossing the street and entering the bakery.

"Welcome! What can I get for you?" a woman behind the counter asked with a smile.

"It smells amazing in here! I'm going to a friend's for dinner and wanted to bring something for dessert. Can I get a variety of things?" Elliot asked.

"Of course. Do you want to pick, or if you're comfortable with telling me who they are, if they live in town, I can pick their favorites?" the woman offered.

"That would be great! Do you know Shaye?" he asked.

"Yes! They're such a wonderful family. I know just what to get them."

Elliot watched as she pulled out a variety of cookies, mini cupcakes and cheesecakes. It all looked and smelled delicious.

"I know I had some of the lemon…Bill! Do we have any of the lemon meringue cupcakes left?" She yelled back to the kitchen area.

A man poked his head through the open doorframe. "I have about half a dozen back here. How many you need?"

The woman looked at Elliot, a question on her face.

"Lemon meringue cupcakes?" he questioned, curious to see what those looked like.

Bill brought out a tray filled with gorgeous cupcakes. They had a cake base, a lemon curd, and a torched meringue topping.

"Those look amazing! I never would have thought to make something like that," Elliot said.

"Are you a baker?" the woman asked.

Elliot nodded. "I do mostly internet orders right now. One day, hopefully, I'll get my own store."

"Here, try this," she said, handing him a cupcake.

Elliot peeled back part of the wrapper and took a bite. The slight sweetness of the cake and the meringue balanced perfectly with the tartness of the lemon curd. There was the right amount of meringue, just enough to taste but not over-powering. It was one of the best things he had tried in a long time.

"These are amazing! The sweetness and tartness are balanced perfectly."

"Thank you," she said, beaming. "I came up with them for Doc's birthday. He loves lemon, although Emma loves them too. I'm Mary by the way," she said.

"Elliot. I'll take the rest of them and whatever else you think they might want. It's my first time meeting everyone besides Shaye and I don't want to show up empty-handed," he said.

"I'll fix you up," she said with a grin, filling a second box with the cupcakes. He finished the one she had given him, glad he had come in. He couldn't wait to try the other things.

Mary rang him up and he swiped his card before grabbing the boxes. "Thank you so much. I can't wait to try every-thing," he told her, smiling. He wasn't quite sure how he would make a living here with such a great bakery already established, but he figured he could keep doing his mail orders. Not quite what he wanted, but he also didn't want to compete with another bakery, especially one run by such nice people.

He window-browsed the rest of the main street, sensing magic at a couple more places. The Winged Potter had some great pieces and he made a mental note to come back and send something home for his mom. There were quite a few pieces in the window that he thought she would like and there was a leather-wrapped-handle knife that he thought Baz would love. His birthday was coming up in a few months and it would make a great gift.

The bookstore had a café on one side and if he hadn't just eaten a cupcake, he would have stopped in for coffee and a muffin. They looked like the muffins from the bakery, so he figured they probably had supplied them just like they did to the hotel. It looked like another great place to explore later; he didn't want to have to juggle the pastry boxes while looking at books. Looking down the street, he could see the florist next and then the clinic where Shaye worked. He headed back to the hotel to grab a quick shower and a nap before heading over for dinner. Luckily his room had a mini fridge to store the cheesecakes.

3

E lliot pulled up to the metal gates, about to pull out his phone to call Shaye, when they suddenly opened. He saw a small camera at the code box and figured they saw him pull up. As he drove up to the front of the house, using the circle driveway to pull all the way around, he saw Shaye waiting for him on the front porch. Once his car was parked, she was running over to him. Jumping out of the car, he grabbed her in a hug. It had been too long since they had seen each other in person, video calls and texts weren't the same. He hadn't realized just how much he had missed her.

"I missed you," he said, holding her tight.

"I missed you too," she said.

He could feel a calming energy from her, and his nerves disappeared.

"Come inside and meet everyone. Well, almost everyone. Gage and Marco usually make it to Sunday dinners, but they're working on a case and won't make it tonight," she explained.

Elliot walked with her, noticing a very large dog watching him carefully from the front porch.

Shaye followed his line of sight and smiled. "That's Rockefeller. He looks scary, but he's very friendly once he knows you're safe. He's protective of us."

Elliot hung back a little bit behind Shaye as they walked up the steps.

"Hey, Rock. Come meet my friend Elliot. He's good," Shaye said.

Elliot held his hand out to sniff, watching as the dog looked at Shaye and then wagged his tail before sniffing his hand. He got a headbutt to his hand and then the dog turned around to go back inside.

"Ready to meet the rest?" Shaye asked.

Elliot nodded, although based on the sounds coming from inside there were a lot of people. "Oh! Hold on. I forgot the boxes in the car," he said, running back to grab the bakery boxes.

"You found the bakery! Aren't they amazing? Mary and Bill are great and they have delicious stuff," Shaye said, leading him into the house.

There was a tall man with dark hair and striking blue eyes waiting for them by the door.

"Elliot, this is my Rolf. Rolf, this is my friend Elliot," Shaye introduced them.

He shifted the boxes to one arm, holding his right hand out to shake. "Nice to meet you. Thanks for having me."

Shaye took the boxes from him, walking toward the kitchen. "Come meet the rest!"

The sounds got louder as they got closer. They certainly all seemed happy to be together. He recognized Marge from the library and the boy, and Tess from when he had met her years ago when she visited Shaye when she worked in his hometown.

"Everyone, this is Elliot. Elliot, this is Rolf's mom Emma and her husband Doc. He's also my boss and the town doctor at the clinic. This is Sam and Tess, who I think you might remember. Sam owns the Black Wolf Brewery. This is Ian and

Berkley. Berkley has the Winged Potter and Ian has been my friend since high school, so I've probably mentioned him before. He does great blacksmith and leather work. And this is Marge, the main librarian, Jimmy, and Duncan. Gawain and Merri will be down in a minute, he's researching something and found a new lead. He's an archeologist. Merri helps him and she's also a librarian."

Elliot did his best to remember the names. "Nice to meet you all," he said. He could sense magic all around this house and knew he needed to bring it up to Shaye sooner rather than later.

"Come grab some food," Emma encouraged. "We're pretty relaxed around dinner, so take what you want. We always have plenty."

As they sat at the table, Elliot let the sounds wash over him. They were all chatting about their day and it was so nice to be part of a family dinner again. It hadn't been that long since he left home, only a few days, but he hadn't realized how much he had missed it.

"Shaye said she got the cheesecake recipe from ye for Christmas. It was delicious," the man next to him said. Ian, he thought.

"Thanks. I'm glad you all liked it. You're Ian?" he asked to confirm. When he nodded, Elliot asked, "Were those your knives I saw in the window at the pottery shop?"

"Aye. I hae a few of my things there. I do a lot of online sales, but Ber keeps some of my pieces there to sell."

"They look great. I saw one I'm going back for to get for my cousin for his birthday," Elliot said.

"Which one? I can set it aside for ye."

"It had a leather-wrapped handle, in the front window, right side," Elliot told him.

"Ah, I know which one that is. I'll grab it out of the window tomorrow for ye," Ian said.

"Thank you," Elliot replied. "Both of your goods look

incredible. I can't wait to come in and find something when it's close to my mom's birthday."

Berkley leaned over to Ian to talk to him. "If you have something specific in mind, let me know. I can do a custom piece for you if you don't find something that matches what you have visioned."

"Thank you," Elliot said. He was touched that they were willing to be so welcoming; the majority of them had never met him.

Elliot helped clear the table and followed everyone into the family room. He took one of the single chairs and watched as the family found what looked like their usual seats. Ian sat on the floor between Berkley's legs, Tess sat on the loveseat with Sam, her legs draped over his lap, Shaye and Rolf were on the couch along with Emma and Doc. He took a good look at his friend; she looked much more relaxed and easy in her own body. Before, having so many people and emotions around her would have been overwhelming after a short amount of time. He was happy to see her being able to enjoy spending time with her family.

Rolf took Shaye's hand and lifted it to his lips for a kiss, making Elliot smile. He was glad his friend had found herself a nice mate.

"I know you're staying at the hotel in town, but you are more than welcome to stay here, if you would like. We have plenty of room. There's no pressure; if you feel more comfortable staying in town and having some space from our crazy loudness, I completely understand," Rolf said with a smile.

Elliot took a moment to come up with his response. It was a very generous offer, considering they thought he was a regular human. Well, he was a regular human, but he had knowledge of paranormals. It spoke well of this found family of Shaye's.

"I would like to stay here, but I feel like I need to confess something first," Elliot admitted. "I don't want to be a burden or to cause you issues by being here. I would love to get to know you; I know you're all good people since Shaye has adopted you all as her family. I don't want you to have to hide who you really are from me.

"I know you're all paranormals; although other than Rolf and Shaye being vampires, I don't know what kind you are." Elliot paused.

"May I ask how you know this?" Rolf asked cautiously.

Elliot noticed Berkley and Tess were sitting up, more alert. He wondered if they were the magical elements he sensed when he came into the house.

"I'm human, but my adopted family isn't. I was raised in a vampire family. They told me about you and Shaye."

"Is that why you stayed near home so often? Shaye seemed quite surprised when you called and said you were coming for a visit," Tess asked.

"It is. My mother is a little bit...overprotective. Both because I'm human and also because she's been convinced there are sketchy things happening in the paranormal community that the Convocation is ignoring. It's caused her to keep me close to home," Elliot replied. He noticed a lot of looks going around the room. He could swear that there was an unspoken conversation taking place that he wasn't privy to.

Shaye leaned forward. "We've had several issues with an increase in hunter activities, both close to home and abroad. Our local Sheriff is also the paranormal Warden for this area. He's been investigating the rise of hunters and the connection to a Convocation member with the help of another Warden and some of the Clan. We've been successful at identifying the Convocation member and two others who were helping him. Convocation member Barry currently has a warrant out for his arrest. He's gone into hiding, although the other two have been arrested. It's still ongoing, which is why you're not going meet Gage or Marco tonight, the other two unofficial members of our family. They got called away to another site to assist.

"The town has a ward over it, reaching even the outlying areas and farms. The ward is to keep those who mean harm out, which keeps hunters and Barry away. We had an incident not that long ago before the ward, where Barry came into town with a bunch of his followers and kidnapped Marge to force her to let them into the paranormal room at the library. He was after a special book that had been sent to her. We've learned some horrible things about what he's been doing," Shaye said.

"I know you're very close to your family but before we talk about anything further, I need you to swear to keep this to yourself. We have a ward here to keep both people who mean harm out, but also to keep them from using any means to listen in. It acts as a silencing dome as well. Without a similar protection on phone lines or on our families' homes, the information could be intercepted by Barry or those working with him," Rolf interjected.

"I'll keep it quiet," Elliot vowed. He wondered what could have happened that they were so worried.

Another blonde woman slipped into the room, sitting near Emma and Doc.

"What'd I miss? There's no way Gawain is tearing himself away right now. He's finally found the link he needs to track down a suspicion he's had," the woman said.

"Merri, this is my friend Elliot. Elliot, this is Merri. She's also a town librarian, has the Paranormal History Museum, and is Tess's sister."

After they both greeted each other, Rolf spoke up.

"We were about to tell him what's going on with the hunters and the Convocation."

He sat there in stunned silence as he listened to their stories. Ian had been attacked, Marge kidnapped, the poor boy also taken and kept for his powers. Elliot was amazed that something like this could have gone on for so long. He wondered how they tracked it so far back and had a feeling they weren't telling him everything. Which was fine; he was a stranger to most of them. Passing through their wards meant he didn't mean them harm, but completely trusting him would take time and friendship. Once he was able to tell his mom, he knew the rest of the family would never hear the end of it. She'd been saying something was hinky at the Convocation for years.

"I'm not sure what I can do to help," Elliot finally said. "But if I can in any way, please let me know. I'll keep this quiet, but I do believe my family may be able to help. I know you all are worried about the phone security, but we have a code that I can use to let them know I need help, and someone will come down. I can give them the message within the town lines, they can bring it back home, Uncle can cast a silencing spell to keep the information safe there. Each of them has a lot of contacts and friends. Some of my cousins have friends in the Convocation and amongst the Wardens as well, so they could at least keep an ear out to make sure there aren't any others.

"My aunt is a Seer, which is why I'm here. Not that I didn't miss you and want to see you," he reassured Shaye, "but she's had a vision for years that I had to stay human and would leave home when the time was right. They kept me safe in the only way they knew how, by keeping me close to home and being overprotective, until she saw it was time for me to go. I didn't even know the Clan was here until she told me. But if she knows to keep an eye out for certain types of things, it might help too."

4

G age was extremely frustrated. He just wanted to go home and sleep in his own bed. He missed the Sunday dinner at the Clan home and was instead eating fast food. He had gotten spoiled, he admitted to himself. There was a reason he wasn't a traveling Warden like Marco; he preferred to stay near his home roost.

"This is a mess," Marco said in disgust.

Gage nodded and couldn't disagree. It looked like an old holding area, clearly not used anymore, but there was still evidence of people being held against their will. Chains were in some of the rooms, the windows all too small to climb out of in a normal human form. There were still the faint smells of urine and waste in some of the rooms with suspicious piles in the corners. Gage wasn't going near those. Some of the walls had scratches, either from nails scratching or a count of days. It was hard to tell. This place didn't look like it had power, running water or plumbing. He wasn't sure how they would have kept warm in the winter. Although this part of South Carolina didn't get a lot of snow, it still got cold. Without a source of heat, even paranormals could die of hypothermia. Especially the more human ones like witches.

"Let's see if we can't find some clue as to where they went. I don't think this was set up as a long-term holding facility. There's just no way. If he wanted to keep them alive, they would need better care. I'm not entirely sure how this was so close to my territory and I didn't know about it," Gage said, angry with himself.

"You have no idea how long it's been vacant. I would guess long before this became your zone," Marco said.

"Yeah. But still… How many of these are hidden away that no one knows about? Statistically, he had to have messed up at least once. Left a clue or something behind," Gage reasoned. "No one is perfect."

Marco nodded. "There's bound to be an office or personal quarters for Barry or his dad here. He's collecting people for their abilities. There's no way he simply collects them and leaves them alone. He's going to visit, make them use their abilities, try to get them to breed, run tests. Something. He would want his own space to take notes or keep the data he collected at each location."

Gage grunted an agreement and ducked his head to fit through the doorway. He sent his magic ahead, looking for any traps or spells they could accidently trigger. Moving slowly, he walked through the hallway, checking each room for magic before Marco went in to search.

"Hey. Take a look at this," Marco said, holding something in his hand.

Gage looked down, noticing the dried plant in his brother's hand.

"This isn't native to here, is it?" Marco asked.

"No, I don't think so. I'm not sure exactly what it is, but it's not something I recognize." He snapped a picture, sending it off to Marge, Merri, and Gawain to research. It didn't have much of a scent anymore. He took other pictures so they could document for the investigation and placed it in an evidence bag. He wanted there to be so much evidence linking Barry to the crimes that there was no way he could not be found guilty. They already had Jimmy's and Marge's testimonies, but he wanted to find every scrap there was. This guy had been a problem for much too long. They still needed to find where the main location was. He could only hope that Barry's greed for having the unique paranormals would keep him from killing them, unlike the people who participated in the voluntary breeding camps.

On one hand he was always sorry to see a death, but on the other hand, he didn't really have much sympathy for people who would take money to have a child and then sell that child to Barry. Who does that? He could only hope that Barry spared the children. They hadn't found any at the camps, although there were signs of baby gear and toys. Jimmy couldn't have been the only one. He needed to talk to the Convocation to set up trusted families to take in any children that were found as a result of the voluntary breeding program.

MERRI: Can you bring a piece home? We can test it to see what kind it is.

GAGE: Sure. Hopefully will be home in a few days. Sean is in charge of the police station while I'm gone, but he's human so he can't do much about the paranormal stuff. If there's a problem, call me. I didn't think I'd be gone more than a day.

MERRI: Just be safe. You and Marco reach out if you need help too.

Gage sent back a thumbs-up emoji and put his phone away.

"Merri wants a piece to test," he explained. "And to tell us to reach out if we need help."

Marco briefly grinned before checking out the next room.

They searched the entire building, but other than finding a small graveyard in the back, they didn't find anything else of interest. There was what used to be an office, papers long since destroyed by water and mildew, while some even looked like they had been set on fire. The ones that they could read, didn't seem to allude to much other than a feeding and "activities" schedule. Gage wondered if the "activities" were sex, or if it would be having them prove out their abilities to Barry. They documented everything, sealing what they could in special bags to help preserve them until the labs would take possession and do their own tests. Gage took a small piece of the plant and put it in a different bag so he could bring it home. He would make a note in the file that he took it for testing. At this point, he would rather have the people he trusted test it than the Convocation, but he also knew he needed to run this investigation through the Convocation and have everything as tight as he could make it for the case. This was a once-in-a-lifetime event, and considering how long they all lived, that was just how he wanted it. He'd prefer this never happened again.

"I think we've exhausted everything inside. Let's check the outside one more time and then we can drop this stuff at the office so the lab techs can see what they can find," Marco said. "Maybe we'll get lucky and find something else out of place."

As the sun started to set, Gage let his magic flow over the area, searching one last time for anything to help them. There was nothing. Barry certainly kept his shit contained.

"Nothing. You?" he asked Marco, sighing as Marco shook his head. "Let's drop this off then. Can I stay at your place tonight? I don't think I'll make it back home tonight." It was late and he was tired. It would be nice catching up with his brother anyway, even if they just sat there and grunted at each other. He did miss having him close.

"Yeah, of course. I'll order pizza. There's a great new place that opened recently. I think you'll like it. I have the pull-out couch, if that works?" Marco asked.

Gage nodded, putting their evidence into his backpack

before shifting to his griffin form, his claws holding the bag. As soon as Marco became his gargoyle, they flew. Over the years, they had found the perfect range of airspace to keep out of human eyes at night, but also avoid the bigger airplanes. Sometimes they had to dodge the smaller ones, but for the most part this was the perfect height. Maybe they could join the Nightwood Clan on their next run. There were several flyers; Gawain would be a little more limited on height, but Doc and Duncan could probably reach their levels. Of course, within the town boundaries, especially on Rolf's land, they were safe so they could fly lower than usual. It would be nice to be part of their run.

They stopped at Marco's house, which wasn't far from the Convocation headquarters. Gage shifted back to human form and grabbed his car from the garage. He was still hiding his shifter side from the Convocation. He didn't fully trust all the members, even after getting rid of the three they knew had been corrupt. By the time they pulled into the lot, he was starving. The building had a helicopter landing pad, which could be used for actual helicopters, but was mostly used by flight-based paranormals. Normally that was how Marco got to work, but today they parked and walked to the front door. One of their allies met them there.

"Tom," Gage greeted him. "It wasn't much. A few papers may be salvageable, a piece of a plant we didn't recognize in a holding room, but that's about it. I took a small part of the plant to have it tested. The rest is in the evidence bags."

"It makes sense to have multiple opinions on it," Tom agreed. He'd been a longtime ally of the brothers and one of the few they knew they could trust. "I'll walk you in."

Gage looked at him and Tom rolled his eyes. Ah. One of the other members must have been raising a stink about something.

"Anything I need to be concerned about?" he asked softly.

Tom wiggled one of his hands back and forth. "Maybe?

Seems like there's a member on the Convocation that is questioning everything again," he said quietly. It was almost a whisper.

"Who?" Marco asked angrily, but also kept his voice down.

"Brandon. He's one of the youngest ones, also has issues maintaining his lifestyle. Not a problem before now, but he's suddenly raising a fuss over Barry. He was all for arresting him earlier, but now seems to be backpedaling. I can't prove it yet, but I'm positive Barry got to him. All it would take was the threat of a little violence or some cash for Brandon to do what Barry wants. He's never really been in a fight, pampered most of his life, got the position when his dad decided to step down and retire," Tom explained. "Anyway, document everything as well as you can and have one of us escort everything to evidence. More witnesses, all that jazz."

Gage took that to mean use the Convocation members they trusted to ensure the chain of evidence was maintained and that there were other witnesses besides themselves that anything they brought in was actually checked into the office. He was glad he had taken photos of everything for himself and was bringing the plant piece back to Tennessee. If evidence started going missing, he would know where to look first.

"We can do some searching into his bank statements and recent history and see if we can connect him. We need to get Barry before he corrupts more members."

"Although maybe it's good. Brandon may have been a weak link later. If we can weed them all out now, at least we know we'll be able to trust the rest," Tom said, holding the door open for them.

"Eric, great to see you. Gage and Marco found some evidence they need to check in. From here on out, any evidence brought in by Gage or Marco doesn't get seen or touched without someone signing for it. As soon as someone requests it and/or signs for it, you and whoever else is here, need to email or text me right away. Date, time, what they wanted, who they are, their title. All of it. If you can get a picture of them, even better," Tom said.

Eric's eyes were wide. "Is this because of—"

"Yup," Tom interrupted. "No matter their position, they have to sign for it. Understand?"

"Yes, sir. I'll make sure it's posted, but I'll keep it vague and say it's for all evidence under a new policy. I'll verbally tell my team the specifics. That way there's at least a reminder posted and if someone is snooping, it won't be obvious what it's about," Eric offered.

"Thanks. Actually, let me get you a list of Wardens this will apply to. There are a few others on the case that I trust."

Gage and Marco followed Tom back out to the front. "I'll keep you informed if I hear anything else. I'll use our code if things get dicey."

Gage nodded. "Same here. Stay safe," he said, shaking Tom's hand before leaving and driving back to Marco's home. It wasn't huge, just a one-bedroom, one-bath home in the middle of the woods, but it suited his brother since he wasn't home very often. The living room was a good size, even when the couch was pulled out.

"I sent the pizza order as soon as we left, so it should be here soon. Luckily they deliver out here; I don't feel like peopling anymore," Marco said, dropping to the couch.

"I hear you. Why do people have to be such assholes?" Gage asked.

"Well, if they weren't, we'd be out of a job," Marco pointed out.

"I'd still have one," Gage smirked. He enjoyed his Sheriff's job; especially now with the ward around the town. It had cut down on incidents and he felt comfortable leaving the town in the hands of his few deputies. Not that he didn't trust them, but they were both human and with the wards in place it meant that they wouldn't have to deal with paranormals causing trouble.

"Yeah, yeah. I was thinking. Maybe when this case is finished, maybe I'll look into moving closer," Marco said, looking at him out of the corner of his eye.

"That would be cool. Where are you looking?" Gage said, excited at the possibility of having his brother closer. Marco could teleport, so he could get to work pretty easily.

"Rockfort," Marco replied. His eyes were cautiously hopeful. Like Gage would ever turn him down.

"I'd love for you to be closer. I miss seeing you," he told his brother, bumping his shoulder against his. "You know Rolf would let you stay at the house, if you wanted to."

Marco nodded. "I know, but I think that I need my own space. I love the thought of being close to them, and I know they consider us part of their family. Which I do too at this point, but it's just been the two of us for so long, and then we were on our own for a bit too. I think having a separate space and being able to go to Sunday dinners or the grill-outs when I can people, would be better. I still have plenty of times that I just need space, and while I think they would do their absolute best to honor that, it's still a lot of people in one area."

"No, I get that. I'm keeping my house and have a similar plan. I see a lot of them in town during the day too, so it's not like I won't see them. Rolf is very laid-back for a Clan leader. He wants everyone to be happy. It's a good trait to have," Gage said.

Marco jumped up when the doorbell rang, bringing back the smell of warm dough and melty cheese. Gage suddenly realized how hungry he was and dove in.

5

Elliot was in the middle of writing down a new recipe idea when he heard Shaye and Tess come home. He had been settling in this past week, having moved in after his first visit. He had stayed that night in the hotel and then repacked his bag and moved into one of the empty rooms in the Clan home. He was holding off on sending for the rest of his stuff; Elliot knew he was going to stay in town, but he had a feeling that it wouldn't be in the large home. He had no idea why, but that was what his gut was telling him and he had no desire to move things twice. He had enough in these suitcases to keep him for a while.

"Hey, Elliot!" Shaye said, coming over to give him a hug. "It smells delicious in here. What did you make?"

"I'm trying a new cookie. Lemon ginger. I think it's close, but not quite there. What do you think?" he asked, handing them each a cookie.

He watched both of their faces as they ate. They seemed to like them.

"They're really good," Tess said, "but I can see what you mean. Like a little something would make them amazing, not just really good. Of course, I'll eat several just like this," she reassured him.

"Maybe a drizzle of glaze?" Shaye suggested.

"Ooo! A lemon glaze would be amazing, not too sweet," Tess agreed, happily grabbing another cookie.

"I can make one real quick," Elliot said, grabbing the ingredients. It sounded perfect. "Don't eat all the cookies so we can try some with the glaze," he warned, smiling. It was fun having someone to bounce his ideas off. "How was work?" he asked them.

"It was pretty quiet today. Not too many people came in. It'll pick up soon though. With school back in session and cold and flu season coming soon, we'll get busy," Shaye said.

"I forgot the bread!" Tess suddenly blurted out before running back out to the garage. When she came back in, she was carrying a couple loaves of sourdough, from what Elliot could tell of the bread bags.

"We stopped on the way home. Rolf was going to throw a soup in the slow cookers this morning, and bread sounded good," Shaye said.

"You think bread always sounds good," Elliot teased.

Shaye smiled and shrugged, not really able to deny that. "Maybe. But they make such nice stuff! Plus, it's good to support local business."

Elliot and Tess laughed. Although both of those statements were true, he had noticed the people in this house loved their sweets and breads and probably contributed to half of the sales at the bakery.

"I'm worried they might move though; their daughter had a baby not too long ago and she lives out of town. They took a trip to visit them and really enjoyed it. I think they might be thinking of closing the bakery and moving there," Tess said. "I don't blame them for wanting to be closer to their family, but we certainly would miss them. And the town doesn't have another bakery. Even the bookstore's café gets most of their stuff from Bill and Mary."

Elliot was surprised how sad and disappointed that made him. It was a great shop and it would be a shame if it closed. "Maybe I can offer to work there and free up time for them to travel more to visit. I love baking every day, and I've been grateful to be able to use your kitchen, but I would love to be able to use professional-sized equipment."

Emma walked in and gently patted his arm. "I think that's a great idea. I can't wait to see what you come up with. Everything you've made has been incredible. I've been smelling these cookies and wanted to see if I could sneak one before everyone else comes home," she said with a grin.

"You're just in time. Tess and Shaye helped me come up with an idea to make them better and you'll get to try it first," Elliot said, handing her a freshly drizzled cookie. "It's not set yet, so the glaze might be a little messy," he warned.

"Oh! These are delicious! I love the combo," Emma said, taking another bite and daintily licking the icing off her fingers. "You should take a couple of these over to Mary and have Shaye introduce you, let them know you're interested in a job."

Elliot chewed on his bottom lip. "You don't think that will be weird? If I just show up?"

"Tell them I sent you," Emma said, smiling. "I think they'll be relieved to have some help."

Elliot nodded and pulled out a small cookie box and packed a few cookies. The first ones he had drizzled were just set enough. Shaye grabbed her keys. "We've got some time, we might as well go now when the cookies are super fresh," she said, sharing a look with Emma and Tess. Weird. He could swear they were having a conversation that he couldn't hear.

"Is it important for me to go right now?" Elliot asked, curious, as he followed his friend out the door. He didn't mind going, but he was wondering why they seemed to push him out the door so quickly.

"Emma thought so. She knows things, like your aunt," Shaye explained as they walked down the driveway.

"Ah," Elliot said. That explained it a little bit; although not why there was such a hurry for him to get there. Maybe they really were thinking of selling and this was the exact right time to offer help so they didn't. Who knew?

"What do you think of the town so far?" Shaye asked. "Have you made it around yet? I can show you my favorites this weekend if you wanted. I'm sorry I've been working the last couple of days. Tess and I are the only nurses at the clinic, so it can make it a little challenging to take time off."

"No, no. Don't feel bad about that. You're helping people. I also didn't give you a lot of notice that I was coming down. I've had lots of fun using the big kitchen in your house. I've seen some of the town, but I would love to see your favorite parts. You can tell me all the details about how you met everyone too. It seems like you finally found your family," he said, looking over at her.

"I did," she said happily. In a quieter voice, she added, "I have better control over my abilities since I turned, too. Which makes it so much better working in town."

"I'm glad," Elliot replied, wrapping an arm around her for a quick side hug. He had seen the effects of her healing and empathic abilities before, and they could take a devastating toll on her. She seemed so much better, even surrounded by people. He was glad that Fate had done right by his friend.

"How's your family doing? Were they upset about you coming here?" Shaye asked. She had witnessed how overprotective his family had been during her stint in his hometown.

"They're good. Mom was a bit of a mess when I left. Apparently, the whole family knew one day I would be sent away," Elliot replied, still feeling a little angry about that. He felt like they had kept things from him, things that directly impacted his life. Shouldn't he have a say in anything?

Shaye reached over, taking his hand, and Elliot felt himself relax. "You know they love you. I think they could have handled it better, but my guess is that they didn't want you to feel unwanted or unloved. If they had told you when you were younger that one day they would send you away, you probably would have felt like they didn't really want you or felt like you were a burden to them," Shaye said softly. "Once they started on that path, when would have been a good time to tell you? If they told you too soon, you would have been chomping at the bit to leave, wondering when it would happen. You would have been miserable with waiting."

Elliot thought about it as they turned onto the sidewalk to walk into town. She might be right. He did have some fears about being left behind when he was young. They had even gone to a family therapist, from what he could remember. As he had grown, he wanted to see new places, and sometimes they did do family trips, but he knew Shaye was right. He would have been unhappy knowing one day he would leave, but not knowing when. Or if he had known the exact date, maybe it would have kept him from fully enjoying the time he had at home.

"Yeah. I can see that," Elliot finally replied. "Do you really think they'll be okay with me randomly coming in and asking if I can work there? It seems a little...pushy? Bold? Not sure what the right word is."

"I do. They've known Rolf and Doc their whole lives. They're one of the families that have been here a long time, and they know about paranormals. Well, the whole town now knows that paranormals exist, but Bill and Mary have known since they were children," Shaye told him.

He really needed to set time aside to talk to Shaye and learn about everything that had happened. He hadn't wanted to push too much when he first arrived because he was new. He didn't want to come across as abrasive.

"Wow. We really need to sit down and talk this all out. It sounds like you've had a lot happen," he said.

Shaye laughed. "A little bit," she agreed, pushing open the door to the bakery. "Mary!" she called out. "I have someone I'd like you to meet!"

Elliot watched as the older woman came out from the back room. She was probably in her sixties, her eyes lighting up as she saw Shaye.

"Hello, again," Mary said to Elliot. "You were just in here! What did you forget?" she teased Shaye.

"I know. We just can't stay away." Shaye smiled. "But this time I have something for you. This is my friend Elliot. We know you guys have been wanting to go back for a visit with your daughter, and Emma thought Elliot here would be a great fit and would give you guys more flexibility for traveling, if you were interested in hiring him. He's an amazing baker and has his own online business, but he's staying here for a while."

"Hi," Elliot said, stepping forward to shake her hand. "I know this seems all out of the blue. I was trying a new cookie recipe today and then they were herding me out the door to meet you," he said, laughing.

"What kind of cookies?" Mary asked.

"Lemon ginger," Elliot replied, holding the box out for her.

"Oh! These are good," Mary said, taking a bite.

"Mary! You need help up front?" a man's voice shouted from the back.

"Nope!" she called back. "Shh, don't tell Bill. I'm eating all of these," Mary said, winking at Elliot.

He grinned back, happy she seemed to like them.

"Emma sent him?" Mary asked.

Shaye nodded. "Tess too. He really is an amazing baker

and I think this would work well for both of you. He gets an industrial kitchen to work in and you guys would have more time to travel. He has a great website with reviews, if you wanted to check it out."

Mary ate another cookie, clearly thinking it over. "You guys knew we were thinking of retiring, didn't you?"

Shaye looked a little sheepish as she nodded. "We don't want to force you guys into something you don't want, so if you're ready to retire, we'll support you in any way we can. We just thought that if you were still deciding, this would give you some thinking room and the ability to see your family more often."

Mary nodded, grabbing a third cookie. "We can give it a trial run, see if we can find a good balance between being here and traveling. This is our home, you know? As much as I really want to be close to my grandbabies, I'd miss the town too. If we decide to retire, would you be interested in buying the business?" she asked Elliot.

He was stunned. He hadn't believed that she would even hire him just because of Emma's and Shaye's say-so, but now she was asking if he would be interested in buying the business she and her husband had owned for years. "I would love to but would probably need time to come up with a loan to cover the amount. Owning my own storefront has always been my dream, and I think I'm meant to be here," he confessed. This had to be what his aunt meant when she said he would find his place. He hoped Bill and Mary stayed owners for as long as they wanted; he would love learning from them.

"Bill, come meet our new employee! He's going to buy it from us when we retire," Mary shouted with a mischievous smile before shoving the last cookie in her mouth and hiding the box in the trashcan.

"What?" An older man leaned around the kitchen door, his hair mostly gray.

Elliot shook his hand when he came over.

"This is Elliot. He's Shaye's friend. Emma thought he would be a good fit and he'd be interested in buying the bakery when we decide to retire. He's going to work here until then, give us the time to travel to see the baby more and decide what we want to do," Mary said, leaning over to give Bill a kiss on the cheek.

Elliot smothered a grin as he saw Bill's nose twitch.

"What did you eat? That's not one of ours. You ate something and didn't share!" Bill asked, his voice offended, but Elliot could see a smirk trying to break free.

"Elliot brought some lemon ginger cookies. They were really good," Mary said, a little smugly.

"Well, I guess we've got to hire him so I get to try them," Bill said. "Welcome aboard."

6

G age was finally going home. He had been away much longer than he had anticipated. After staying the night at his brother's, they had been called back in the next day by Brandon in the Convocation. He could see why Tom was suspicious of him. He wanted a play-by-play of how they found the location, what they found, how exactly they walked through the building, and a whole lot of unnecessary details. Gage was glad that he and his brother had a telepathic link so they could communicate during the interrogation. They kept some of the details quiet, including that they kept part of the plant for separate testing. It was in the report if he really wanted to know.

"Brandon! What is the meaning of this?" Tom had stormed in with other Convocation members. None of them had looked happy.

Brandon had stammered his way through an explanation, saying he wanted to hear about it directly from the investigators so he could ask questions. Tom had sent him on his way and then apologized.

"This should never have happened. We've created a new procedure stating that Convocation members are not allowed to call in investigators for private meetings. It was meant to stop things like this, but we haven't sent the message out to the Wardens yet. I'll make sure that's done today. If he or anyone else tries it again, please call me." Tom had walked them out and had privately added that they were trying to limit how much information Barry could get from the investigation. The procedure called for a minimum of half the Convocation members to be present to talk to an investigator, thinking there was safety in numbers. Even if Barry bribed some of the members, there should be at least one on the team that would be honest and submit a report of the meeting. If information was leaked from that, then they knew where to start looking. If a lone member called a meeting, there could be no report filed and the information would be lost to the other Convocation members, as well as no trace to the traitor.

By the time the day was over, Gage was not in the mood to deal with more people and he had crashed at his brother's house again. But now he was heading home. Marco was coming too, so instead of flying or finding public transportation, Gage would be teleported. He was hoping he could head to Rolf's house and eat dinner there. His deputies weren't expecting him today, so he had the time to check in with the Nightwood Clan.

He needed to be around people he could trust and relax around. The entire time he was at the Convocation he felt like he had to watch everything he did or said. It had always been that way, but since this Barry business, it was even more intense.

They stepped onto the front porch, the lights on inside the house. Gage could already feel himself relaxing. The front door swung open, Shaye standing there with a frown. As they stepped inside, she moved to stand between them, touching them each lightly on the arm. His shoulders dropped as the last of the tension melted away.

"Come in and get something to eat. Relax. You can tell us all about it later," she ordered.

Gage and Marco exchanged a smile. When they first met Shaye there was no way that she would have ordered them about. She certainly had adopted them into her family. Walking in, they were met with a cascade of noise as the entire family was there; he even saw Gawain, although he did have his tablet with him. They didn't have much time to think, as they were ushered into grabbing dinner. Tonight, it looked like roast with potatoes and roasted vegetables. There were a couple loaves of bread to go with it, already sliced but still warm. He had a large serving, enjoying the chatter of everyone around him. He noticed Marco soaking up the atmosphere too.

As they were clearing the table, Jimmy came over to him. "Uncle Gage, do you have to go again or are you staying here?"

"I'm here for now. I don't know if I'll need to leave again, but for now I'm here. Why?"

"I was hoping I could practice my TruthSpeak with you again. I want to see how far I can make it go to protect every-one," Jimmy replied.

Gage nodded. "We can do that. Maybe you can stop by after school this week? I'll check with Marge and see when would be a good time." He imagined the lingering effects of the unexpected visit from the woman from the Convocation who had attempted to use a TruthSpeaker on them last month was the cause for this. It wouldn't hurt for Jimmy to practice with his powers and if it made him feel more in control, that couldn't hurt either. Jimmy had had so much happen in his life that was out of his power. But he had finally ended up with a family who adored him.

Emma and Doc brought out coffees and teas, and a hot chocolate for Jimmy as they all moved into the living room.

"How did your trip go?" Rolf asked.

Gage sighed. "Frustrating. We found an old holding area, but there wasn't much left. We did find that plant that I sent you a picture of. I'm pretty sure it's not native to here, so I'm hoping it will give us another area to look at. There were a few papers, but nothing really conclusive. It had clearly been emptied before they left.

"The Convocation might have another Barry sympathizer. Our contact, Tom, is suspicious of a guy named Brandon. He voted to investigate and arrest Barry before, but is now questioning everything. They think he may have been bribed. The Convocation has recently made a policy that a single Convocation member is not allowed to interview or take evidence from the Wardens, in an effort to keep information and evidence from disappearing."

"Does that policy extend to civilians?" Sam asked.

"I'll have to ask. It would make sense; the same logic would apply. And it would keep you guys from having another random Convocation member showing up demanding answers," Gage replied. He grabbed his phone and sent a text off to Tom.

"Tess, Merri, and I have been working on figuring out how to best test the plant. I think I can do a spell that will show us the last moments of the piece when it was broken from the main plant, which might show us more of the area it came from. I'm not great at that kind of spell, but it's worth a shot. It won't hurt the plant. Tess and Merri have another spell to tell what kind it is," Berkley said.

"Do you have it with you? We have everything ready. We'd need to do it in the kitchen, the library ceilings are too high," Gawain added.

"I do," Gage confirmed. He wasn't sure what the ceiling height had to do with it, but he trusted that they knew what they were doing.

"Can I go play a video game with Dave? He asked if I could get on tonight," Jimmy asked.

"Is your homework done?" Duncan asked his adopted son. When Jimmy nodded, Duncan said, "Go ahead," smiling as he ran upstairs.

The rest of them headed into the kitchen, where Tess pulled out a large book and set it on the counter.

"Okay, let's see what we have," Gawain said, gently taking the plant from Gage. "I think I've seen this before, out west. It looks like a seed pod, but there are several plants that have those. Anyone else recognize it?"

Everyone shook their heads. He agreed it looked like a seed pod, although that didn't narrow it down very much.

Berkley held out his hand. "May I?"

Gawain handed it over. Berkley cupped it in his left hand, his right hovering over the top. As he muttered some words, a dim glow grew until a beam of light shot up to the ceiling. As Gage tilted his head to follow it, he realized it was creating an image. He grabbed his phone to record. It was a desert-like area, other shrub brush and desert plants around, the seed pod hanging on a small straggly-looking bush or tree. It looked like the bush was dying or hibernating, most of the leaves gone. A human-shaped body brushed against it, the dried edges of the pod catching on their clothing and getting pulled from the plant. As the image zoomed out, they could see Barry dragging the person who brushed against the plant. Gage couldn't tell if they were injured or drugged, but they were stumbling along, barely shuffling their feet.

The image cut off. If the person was imprisoned by Barry, either Barry had just hunted down the person or he was bringing him to a holding area.

"Sorry. I was hoping it would show more than that. I'm not very good at that type of spell," Berkley apologized, his voice sounding exhausted. Ian wrapped an arm around him, helping support him. Gage imagined it was a lot of work trying to get something out of an inanimate object.

"No, that was much more than we had before," Marco protested.

"I recorded it and can run the face through a missing persons database. Depending on when it was, at least a sketch might be in the system. It'll give us another location to look at," Gage said. "Thank you."

"Our turn," Tess said, gently taking it from Berkley. She and Merri had an enormous botanical book sitting on the counter. As they touched the tip of the plant into a jar of liquid, the book opened and the pages turned wildly, almost like there was a strong wind shuffling through them.

Gage watched as Shaye lightly touched Berkley's shoulder as she slipped past him to get to the fridge. She pulled out a plate of cheese and crackers and grabbed another container off the counter. Placing it where everyone could reach, but just a little closer to Berkley, she lifted the lid to reveal a bunch of cookies. He waited until Berkley took a few and hummed happily as he found a lemon one. He was still amazed that his favorite cookies seemed to make a regular appearance in the Clan house.

There was suddenly silence, other than people eating, as the book settled down and a couple words glowed on a page. Merri leaned forward. "Desert willow."

Gawain pulled out his phone and a map. Using a highlighter, he filled in some states, it looked like mostly out west and southwest, although it seemed to go all the way to California. Well, it narrowed it down from fifty-one states to eight or nine. He didn't see it being in California. That state was a little too big-brother for Barry to avoid being noticed for that long. He would guess it would be in one of the smaller populated states. Texas had so much land it would be easy to hide there, or even Nevada. Arizona was getting more populated, but New Mexico still had plenty of wide areas of people-free spots. All of them had the desert-like atmosphere described in the one letter Doc had found.

"It helps narrow it down a little bit," Gage said. At least they now knew which states to look in, which was infinitely better than trying to find it in the entire country.

"I'll start searching at night and fly over places," Marco said.

"Do you need a concealment spell?" Berkley offered.

Marco shook his head. "All of these places will be light-free at night and my coloring is pretty dark, so I won't be spotted. I've done this before without any issues, but thank you for the offer."

7

G age pulled into the station, content to be back in his routine. Stepping through the doorway, he rested his hand on his wards, checking them for anything unusual. With the town wards, it probably wasn't needed any longer, but at this point it was habit and part of his routine. Sending his magic through the building, he was happy when it came back to him and reported no changes or attempts to manipulate his protections.

"Welcome back, boss," Sean called out from his desk.

"Thanks. Any problems?" Gage asked.

"Nope, it was all pretty quiet. Mrs. Leiderman locked her keys in the car again. Doug gave the safety speech at the grade school."

"Did he remember the sticker badges this time?" Gage asked. Doug was a great guy, but last year he had forgotten the kid badges. Gage had to run them over because some of the little kids were upset they weren't going to get one and Doug had called him in a panic. The kids had heard all about getting deputy badges from their older siblings who had previously gone through the safety program, and of course preschoolers wanted to be cool deputies like their older siblings had been.

"He did. I don't think he's going to make that mistake again," Sean laughed. "Especially since one of the criers was his own niece after he had hyped up the badges to her beforehand."

"I forgot about that," Gage admitted, shaking his head.

"How was the work trip?" Sean asked.

"Frustrating. Not as productive as I would have hoped," Gage replied. "The guy is great at covering his tracks." He had told his deputies a little bit about what was going on. He didn't want Barry or another sympathizer from the Convocation contacting his deputies when he wasn't there trying to get information. Gage had told them the bare minimum and explained that if any requests for information on Jimmy, Rolf's group, or the town and its people in general came through, to send it directly to him. He had no idea how he would have handled this if the town didn't know about paranormals. It would have made it so much harder.

"He'll mess up somewhere. They always do. If you need to go again, just let us know. The ward makes it so much easier to only have the two of us when you're gone," Sean said.

Gage nodded. "Thanks." He headed to his office, pulling up his emails as he sat down. He had a couple of paperwork items to work on, for both his jobs. Grabbing his thermos, he poured himself a cup of coffee and sat down to catch up.

Around lunchtime, he looked up at the knock on his door. Marge stood there, holding takeout bags from Black Wolf Brewery and the bakery.

"Hey, I didn't get a chance to talk to you much last night. How are you really?" she asked, sitting down and handing him the bags.

"Okay. Tired. Frustrated we can't find much on this guy to

finally put it to a close. None of us are dumb, there's no way he can keep outsmarting all of us," Gage replied. Rolf was a genius with numbers, Doc had thousands of years' experience, he and Marco were just as old, Gawain had a knack for finding things, Merri was an ace at research. They had all been working on this and he didn't feel like he was any closer to solving it.

Grabbing the dessert first to cheer himself up, a tantalizing smell came from the bag. Bringing it to his nose, he took a deep sniff, his griffin pushing forward.

"Is this a new dessert?" he asked.

Marge was looking at him oddly when he looked up. "Lemon ginger cookies. Mary and Bill have some new help in the bakery. Remember Shaye's friend Elliot, who was coming for a visit? They hired him so they can see the grandbaby more often. I have a feeling he might settle here long-term though. Anyway, he makes some amazing desserts. Those are one of his creations."

"Hmm. I love lemon," he muttered around a bite of cookie. It was perfect and he was going to devour all four cookies.

"How's the museum going?" he asked after he swallowed the last one.

"Good. Steve's been in there about once a week with a new question. The poor man came in and was reading mpreg books and was too embarrassed to ask his mate if that was a possibility," Marge said.

"What's mpreg?" Gage asked, grabbing his burger.

"Male pregnancy," Marge replied.

Gage choked on his bite, grabbing his coffee to wash it down. "What?"

"It's a trope in some romance books. Apparently Steve has been reading a few gay paranormal romance books and came across the mpreg trope and wanted to know if it was a real thing. He said he was not ready to have kids," Marge told him, her eyes laughing.

"Oh my gods. Can you imagine?" Gage shook his head. "Why didn't he ask Marshall? I thought they completed the mating bond and were good?"

"He said he didn't want to offend Marshall if it was true by insinuating that he didn't want his kids," Marge said. "I think he was trying to keep from hurting Marshall's feelings. It was quite the conversation. Of all the things I thought would be asked, that was one I never saw coming."

"Yeah. I think there's going to be some oddball questions, especially from humans. There's so much misinformation out there," Gage said, offering Marge a fry.

"Thanks. You should come over for dinner tonight," she said.

Gage thought about it, but he really just wanted to fall asleep. "Probably not tonight. I just want to fall into my own bed. Maybe in a couple of days." He also hated feeling like he was imposing just because he was lonely.

Marge gave him a look. "You're not imposing. Dork. You've been adopted in, just like I have. Don't wait long." She stood up, Gage following suit. Marge gave him a quick hug before she left to go back to work.

Male pregnancy. Good grief. Thank goodness that wasn't a real thing. He saw what his mother went through when she was pregnant with Marco. No thank you.

Three days later, Gage found himself outside of the Nightwood Clan home. His griffin was being a pushy bastard lately. Gage normally kept his visits to once a week, because he was still getting used to having a larger family.

"Come on in. We decided to grill today, since it's still nice out. They're all in the back," Ian said as he led the way through the house. "Do ye prefer burgers or chicken? We've got both."

"I like either," Gage said, wishing he thought to bring something.

As he walked through the kitchen, he saw Shaye and Emma putting together a topping platter. "Can I help with anything?" he asked, pausing as Ian went out to the back.

"Do you want to unpack the desserts onto this tray?" Shaye asked, handing him a bakery box and an empty platter.

Gage drew in a deep breath, noticing the same tantalizing scent. He eagerly opened the box, but didn't see the lemon cookies.

"What's wrong?" Shaye asked, coming over to him.

"Oh. Nothing. Marge brought me these amazing lemon ginger cookies earlier and I thought I smelled them in here, but I don't see any," Gage said, feeling silly about being disappointed over cookies.

"You smelled the same smell?" Emma asked. "Those are great cookies. I love the icing."

Gage nodded, focusing on trying to make the tray look nice, not just like he dumped the cookies out.

Shaye and Emma exchanged a look over his head, which he missed.

"You know what? I think I forgot to buy enough buns. Gage, would you be willing to go to the bakery and grab some rolls or buns?" Shaye asked.

"Yeah, sure. I'll be back in a couple of minutes. Do you need anything else?" he asked, finishing up the cookies.

"No, I think that's it," she answered, smiling.

He wasn't quite sure why she looked so happy all of a sudden. Not that she had looked unhappy before, but she was beaming at him. Maybe she had been really worried about the buns? He had felt bad for not bringing anything, so this was perfect.

He decided to walk to the bakery instead of messing with the car and the gate. It was nice out and he could stretch his legs after being at his desk so much. The bakery was due to close in a half hour, but he should be there in time. If they didn't have any left, he could always run down to the grocery store and grab some generic ones.

Gage reached out to grab the handle of the bakery's door, not seeing Bill or Mary inside. The bell chimed as he entered announcing his arrival. His nose was filled with the same scent he had smelled earlier, but he didn't see the cookies in the case. He would have bought them all and saved them for later. Maybe he could ask if they had any in the back. Walking closer to the case, his griffin surged forward, trying to take over.

Knock it off, Gage told his animal side. *It's too small in here and Mary will smack me if you destroy her shop.*

Mine. The griffin stated, still pushing forward but not enough to take over his form.

What are you going on about? Gage asked.

His whole body froze as a new voice shouted out from the back room and he took a deep inhale, soaking in the scent.

Mate.

8

"Be there in just a second!" Elliot called out from the kitchen. He was just pulling out a tray of rolls. He was hoping Shaye's group could give them a taste test today. They were herb infused and he wanted to make sure they weren't too strong. Or too subtle for that matter.

Pulling the oven mitts off, he tossed them on the counter after setting the rolls on a cooling rack and shutting off the oven. He had enough baked goods ready for tomorrow and more were sitting in the fridge waiting to bake in the morning. He sent a picture to his mom, showing her the large kitchen. He had been trying to keep her up to date with what was going on as much as possible, at least as much as he could without saying anything about the Convocation.

Walking through the doorway, he stopped as he saw a large man standing there. He had caramel-colored skin, short black hair with a closely cropped beard and mustache. Facial hair normally didn't do it for him, but on this man it was making his body take notice. His eyes were framed by long lashes, the color a pretty gray. He was huge. Standing well over six feet, probably around six feet seven inches, if he had to guess based on the height of the guys in Shaye's family.

The light blue t-shirt he was wearing was straining around his biceps, the muscles large and well developed. It was also snug enough that Elliot could tell he had washboard abs, and he was suddenly overcome with the urge to lick them. The man's hands were large, a few old-looking scars across the tops, some scattered around his arms. He had nice kissable lips, Elliot thought.

He watched as the man's eyes flashed to amber and realized that this was a paranormal. He felt safe though; not because of the wards, he thought it was this man who was inspiring the feeling. Elliot also wanted to climb him like a tree. He was an average height of five feet eleven inches, but he felt small comparatively. He wasn't a big guy, not that tall and certainly not muscular. He was trim, but his muscles were leaner and were from working with sacks of flour and kneading dough.

"Hello, mate. My name's Gage," a deep voice rumbled.

Oh shit. Mate? That would explain why he wanted to lock the door and drag the man into the back room.

"I'm Elliot," he replied. He took a step forward reaching out a hand to shake hello.

He watched as Gage took a deep breath, scenting him. Those coloring-changing eyes closed, his mate visibly trying to get control of himself. That was stupid, he chided himself. None of the paranormal mates he had witnessed finding each other had ever shaken hands and now Gage probably thought he didn't know about paranormals.

"I'm human but I was raised by vampires," he offered quickly. "I know about mates." He didn't want Gage to think he had to hide who he was.

"Elliot? You're Shaye's friend?" Gage asked, wanting to confirm that he actually knew who he was talking to. Having two Elliots at the same bakery would be bizarre, but Gage was feeling off balance. He never expected Fate to give him a mate of his own.

"I am. You know her?" Elliot grabbed his phone and sent a quick text to his friend. Not that he thought he was in danger or Gage was lying to him, especially with his own reaction to the man, but it was always better to double-check.

"I do. I'm the Sheriff, as well as the area's Warden."

Elliot's phone dinged and he smiled as he looked down.

SHAYE: Congratulations on finding your mate! I'm so happy for you. We had a feeling when he mentioned a scent. Come home for dinner and remind him to grab rolls. ;)

ELLIOT: Will do. He's good?

SHAYE: Yes. He's a great guy. He's been good to us. We've adopted him. Not officially because of his Warden status, but he's one of ours.

ELLIOT: We'll be there soon.

He looked up, catching Gage looking at him hungrily.

"Sorry. I was checking with Shaye. It's not that I don't trust you, but…"

"You don't have the same senses I do. I understand. Even if you know about mates, you would want to be cautious," Gage replied.

Elliot nodded. "She said to come back for dinner and to bring the rolls?"

Gage laughed. "That's how they got me to come in. She said they were low on rolls or buns for dinner."

"I just made some. I'm testing out a new recipe. I'll throw them in a box really quick and we can go." He wasn't quite sure what to do with his new mate. Was Gage expecting them to mate tonight? He knew how most paranormal matings went. Fast. Naked and mated the same day. He wasn't opposed to a quick mating, he had seen them his entire life, but he would like to know his mate a little better first. Although he really wanted to explore that giant body.

"Can I help close up?" Gage offered.

"Uh, sure. Thank you. I usually sweep and make sure the

front is clean. I've got the back mostly done except for a few things to wash up."

"I can clean out here," Gage said.

Elliot nodded, pulling out the broom and the spray cleaner he used for the tables and the glass display case. He watched mesmerized as the arm muscles bunched and flexed as Gage cleaned.

A throat cleared, and Elliot looked up to find that Gage had caught him staring. Just how long had he been creeping on his mate?

"Ah, I'm done here. I can help wash the dishes," Gage said, his cheeks tinted pink.

"Yes. Sorry. I didn't mean to stare," Elliot apologized. Well, this mating was starting out awkwardly. Go him.

"It's okay, mate. I don't mind," Gage said, a small smile on his face. "I know humans like to know each other a little more. Would you want to come over to my house tomorrow and we can talk?"

"I'd like that," Elliot replied. He felt a little relieved that Gage was going to take the time to talk to him. Humming softly, he packaged up the still hot rolls, along with a few plain ones that didn't sell earlier in the day. He heard the sounds of water swishing as Gage began handwashing the remaining bowls.

Walking up to the cute Victorian-style home, Elliot felt a little nervous. He had talked to both Shaye and his mom last night. His mom had been thrilled he had a mate but sad because it meant he wouldn't be moving back home. Baz had shouted "Go get it!" and even his aunt had grabbed the phone and told him to get with the mating already. Elliot had hung up pretty quickly after that. He knew mates were supposed to be a perfect match for you and Shaye had nothing but good things to say about Gage. He trusted his friend's judgment, but he selfishly still wanted to talk to his mate and get to know him a little more before jumping into bed with him. Just because they were fated, didn't mean that they didn't still need to communicate and have a good solid foundation for their relationship.

Ringing the bell, he could feel the magic surrounding the house. There were some serious wards around it. He gulped as his mate opened the door wearing a pair of gray sweatpants and another snug shirt. Good lord, that was something, he thought as his cock twitched in his jeans.

"Do you want something to drink? Or eat? I can make something. Not as good as you, but it'd be edible," Gage offered.

Elliot realized that Gage was just as nervous and that put him at ease.

"I'm good for now. Can we talk?"

Gage nodded, leading him into a family room. The wood floors, trim, and molding looked original. It was all in good shape and clean.

"This is a cute house," Elliot said, trying to break the ice. While he never really expected to get a mate of his own, he also never would have envisioned it being so awkward.

"Thanks. I bought it when I got the Sheriff's position. It was a bit of a mess, but I've had fun working on it. Uh. I'm not sure how this is supposed to go," Gage admitted. "I never thought I'd get a mate. I haven't been around many matings."

Elliot looked at him questioningly. He seemed like he was friends with Shaye's group and they were all mated. "You're friends with Shaye and her group though, right?"

Gage nodded, gesturing to the couch for Elliot to sit down. Once Elliot sat, Gage took a seat on the opposite end, turning to face him.

"I am. I have a brother, who is also unmated. We were alone for a long time. I'm friends with Marge, the town's head librarian, and she recently found her mate. We were both kind of loners though, so neither one of us had a lot of experience with relationships. I've vaguely known Rolf, Berkley, Sam, and Doc since I took the Sheriff position. They were all here before me. It was more of a saying hi in passing type of relationship. I kept myself apart for a long time. But when the mates started showing up, the Nightwood Clan formed and they kept pulling me in.

"I try to get over there for Sunday dinners when I can. After being solitary for so long, I still struggle with feeling like I'm not imposing. It's nothing they've done," he rushed to assure Elliot. "It's just me. My brother is the same way."

Elliot nodded to show he was listening. It sounded similar to when one of his cousins had brought in a new member. They had been on their own for so long, they had struggled to adapt to being in a family environment. Now, they were doing just fine, although they did still need some space away from everyone every once in a while, which his family understood. He imagined it was something similar here.

"How long has it been since you've had a family of your own, besides your brother?" Elliot asked. Gage hadn't mentioned any other family members.

"I never knew my father. My mother died a little over two thousand years ago," Gage said so quietly that Elliot had to strain to hear him.

Holy shit. That was...that was old. It would make Gage the oldest paranormal he had ever met. How was it even possible? He knew there were a few that were almost immortal, like the Fae. They claimed they were immortal, but they could still be killed, although it was pretty hard to do. Gage wasn't registering as a Fae, so maybe he was one of the other kind.

"How old are you?" Elliot asked.

"Two thousand and seventeen. I think. I know Marco's age, and I think I was around ten or so when he was born."

"You're the oldest one I've ever met," Elliot said, a little bit in shock.

"There's not a lot of us who are older," Gage admitted. "At least not that I've come across."

"Would you know if they were old?" Elliot asked, interested. He hadn't heard of that ability before. Granted, he didn't get out a ton, but his family loved to talk. Elliot watched as a look came over Gage's face, one he didn't know how to interpret.

"Has Shaye said anything unique about the Nightwood Clan?" he asked.

"No. I don't think so. I know they have all different kinds of paranormals in the Clan, which makes it different from most," Elliot replied. Now he was confused. Was there more going on that he didn't know about? He had heard a lot about the situation with Barry and the hunters, but that was about it. He'd had a feeling that he wasn't being told everything but figured that was because he was the new guy. He had to earn their trust.

"Okay. Give me one minute," Gage said, pulling out his cell phone. "Hey, you're on speaker phone. I'm talking to Elliot and was going to explain why I'm so old, but realized he didn't know about the Clan yet. There are a few other things I need to explain, but it's harder without telling him about the Clan's uniqueness. I wanted to make sure it was alright to let him in on it."

"Oh, no! I thought as his mate, you would want to or should be the one to tell him. Was I wrong?" Shaye asked, concern in her voice.

"No, no. That makes perfect sense; I just wanted to check," Gage replied.

"Of course! He's your mate. Plus, I trust him. He's a good friend," Shaye said.

"Thanks. We'll probably be over with questions later," Gage said.

"Anytime." Shaye hung up and Gage looked back over at his mate. Other than the family, he had never had to tell someone about his shifter side. He knew the Clan would accept him and Marco, but it was a different feeling telling his mate. Elliot was human, so while he might feel the pull of attraction, the mate bond wouldn't be pulling at him as hard yet.

"Is it bad?" Elliot asked. He didn't think they would be involved in anything illegal, but all this secrecy was weird.

"No. At least I don't think so. I hate to ask this, but you can't tell anyone outside of the Nightwood Clan, myself, and Marco. I know that seems extreme, but you'll understand once I tell you. If the information got out, all of us would be in danger," Gage said, internally chastising himself for sounding so melodramatic. But he also wasn't wrong.

"Okay. I can do that," Elliot said. What in the world was he getting himself into?

Gage took a deep breath. "So, some paranormals, like the Fae and dragons, are considered immortal."

Elliot nodded, trying to show he was listening and understood. Gage looked nervous and he didn't want to interrupt.

"It's not a true immortality though. They can still be killed, although it's harder to do. Of course, if they don't have a life-threatening injury, then they could potentially live forever."

"Right, I know that," Elliot responded, still not certain where this was going.

"There are a few paranormals that have true immortality," Gage said in a rush.

"What? How? I've never heard of this before," Elliot replied.

"There are a few paranormals that are one of a kind, generally called rare paranormals. Most people now think they're extinct or were simply stories, even amongst other paranormals. Those rare paranormals have a true immortality. Even if they have a normally life-ending injury, they wouldn't die. It may take a long time, but they would eventually heal from it."

"And someone in the Nightwood Clan is one of these rare paranormals?" Elliot asked.

Gage nodded. He didn't want to spill Doc's secrets, that was up to him to share. "I've collected as much information as I can through my life about these rare ones. I've discovered that they can share their immortality with people they claim as their family, their Tribe or Clan. Whatever their grouping name is."

"And the Nightwood Clan has done this?" He couldn't think of another reason for Gage to be explaining it the way he was.

"They have. I'm sure they'll all introduce you to their shifter sides, but I don't want to presume I have their permission to tell you," Gage said, an apology in his voice.

"No, that makes sense. It's only right to let them choose if they're going to tell me or not," Elliot agreed.

"But the thing is, what you need to know as my mate before we go any farther, is that I'm one too. I can show you my shifter side in the basement, when you're ready," he offered.

He was stunned. First he got a mate, now his mate was immortal and he could be too. This was not anywhere close to what he thought would happen when he learned he was coming to Rockfort. "So, if we would mate, I would get your immortality?" Elliot finally asked.

"Yes. I'm doing this all wrong," Gage said, flustered. He normally was pretty well-spoken and he knew he was intelligent, but that certainly wasn't coming across today.

"Take a breath, and take your time," Elliot told him, reaching out to place a hand on his knee. "I'm listening."

Gage breathed in and held it for a few seconds, letting the air out slowly. "I am a rare paranormal. I shared my immortality with my brother, as he only had the usual type that goes with his species. We don't match species-wise. It seems like Fate only allows one of a kind with the rare paranormals. They can mate, have children, share their immortality, but the children will take after the other parent or after part of the immortal. For example, I knew a witch and a manticore who were mated. Their children were witches and lions."

"Well we're not going to have kids," Elliot joked. "But what does that mean for our mating? I would stay human but be immortal?" That was kind of disappointing. He had hoped that one day he would be able to become a paranormal and be stronger. Being immortal and having a mate was worth giving up that hope, but still.

"That's one option," Gage agreed. His hands were sweaty now. He was nervous about showing his shifter side and having his mate agree to be with him. Now that he knew he had a mate, he was thrilled to know that Fate hadn't forgotten about him.

"What's the other?"

"The Nightwood Clan has a lot of different paranormals. Not all of them could change you, but there are vampires and a werewolf shifter. There is a jaguar shifter as well, but I'm not sure if she has the ability to change humans or not. One of them could change you if you wanted to be a paranormal. The Clan has a few more unique traits that might influence your decision."

"Go on," Elliot encouraged. When he thought he was coming over to get to know his mate, this was not what he was expecting. At all.

"There have been problems with hunters and an old vampire named Vlad. I'm sure your family's heard of him. Anyway, Vlad's been taken care of, but last year Sam had been hit with a death spell by one of his lackeys and the only way to save him was to create a blood oath bond amongst the Clan. It gave them all a telepathic link to each other, which is what Shaye used to help save him. When they created the blood oath bond, it joined them all together and saved Sam, but it also caused some problems with the rare paranormal in the Clan. Their animal side thought this telepathic link was the start to forming their Tribe. To help settle the animal down, eventually everyone completed a ritual that would join them together; it shared the immortality with them all and created another telepathic link, this one being run through the shifter side of the rare paranormal.

"I cannot join the Clan, as it goes against the rules of the Convocation for Wardens. They don't know that I shared my immortality with my brother when he was a child and created my own little Flight of two. I've been adopted into the family regardless and have been told that my mate, whenever I found them, would be welcome to join the Clan/Tribe if they wanted. Whether you decide to stay human or change into a paranormal, I think joining them would be good for you. It would give you a family here and also a safety net with the threat of Barry and the hunters still in play," Gage said.

9

Elliot sat there, a little stunned. What. The Hell. There were two rare paranormals, who were truly immortal, living in the same town. One of which happened to be his mate. What were the odds of that? Maybe his aunt was right, and Fate had brought this all together. It certainly seemed like Fate was drawing people together for something. To fight against Barry, maybe.

"I think I would need to think it over," Elliot said slowly. When he saw the light dim in Gage's eyes, he hurried to add, "Not about being your mate, but which path is best for me. For us. Do you think I could meet your shifter side?"

Gage nodded, holding out a hand to help him off the couch. "I need to go to the basement. I don't fit as well up here and I don't want anyone seeing through the windows either." Even with the town wards, he didn't feel safe shifting in his house where people could see. Now if he was on Rolf's property, that would be different. There were woods to hide in and all sorts of other protective wards. Plus, Berkley could do a cloaking spell. Gage did well with protective ward type of spells, but other ones not so much.

He led the way to his basement, which he had redone to

fit his needs. He had actually dug out more of the basement floor, putting in a new concrete floor and metal beams to support the weight of the house. On one side he had installed a small bathroom. Shelving for storage lined that wall. The rest of the basement on the other side of the steps was his sanctuary when he needed to shift. He had grow lights for his plants, giving it a more garden-like feel. He had a few flowering bushes, some dwarf fruit trees. The middle of the basement was kept bare.

"Can you wait by the base of the stairs? I get a little larger when I shift," Gage said. The room was large enough he could spread out and lazily use his wings to float above the ground. It wasn't the same as flying, but it had worked for him for a long time.

Elliot stood in place, holding on to the railing. Gage didn't tell him what kind of shifter he was, so he was bracing himself for anything. Well, except for a water shifter. There was no water here, other than the sink. He could feel the buzz in the air as Gage's magic shifted, his human body disappearing to have a large, winged beast take its place. Oh my gods. Gage was a griffin. He thought for sure those were myths.

Elliot let go of the railing and walked slowly toward his mate. For the most part, he looked like what the myths portrayed him to be. An eagle head complete with a sharp-looking beak, a mane made of the softest-looking feathers, large feathered wings sprouting from the middle of his back. That part was a little different than most of the pictures he had seen; they had always been shown at the shoulders, which actually would make using his wings and front legs at the same time challenging. It made more sense the wings would be elsewhere. His front legs ended in talons like an eagle, but the legs were thick and muscular, not like a normal bird leg. His dark tawny fur-covered body looked just like a lion, complete with huge back paws and a tail.

He was easily eight feet in length, not including his tail, with a wingspan of twenty-five feet. As Elliot walked closer, he saw that Gage's head stood above his own. He wondered if he would be able to take a flight with him one day.

"Can I touch you?" Elliot asked, his hand out for Gage to scent. He realized he was treating him like a dog and wondered if he was insulting his mate. The large head nodded, his eyes an amber color in this form, watching him carefully. Starting at the top of his head, Elliot realized that instead of earholes like an eagle, Gage actually had small pointed ears. They were covered in feathers and blended in with the rest. His feathers were soft to the touch. Petting his way down Gage's chest, he knelt on the floor to look at his feet. The feathers ran from his head to chest making their way halfway down his front legs where it transitioned into his lion's fur, the talons wickedly sharp. Standing back up, Elliot stroked the soft fur along his mate's back. That would be comfortable to snuggle against, he thought. The back legs were powerful looking, muscular and ending in huge cat paws. Gage's tail was slowly swishing back and forth, looking just like a lion's, even with a tuft of fur on the end.

"You are so cool looking," Elliot said, walking back to Gage's head. He now knew why Gage had all the secrecy up front. If Barry was collecting rare paranormals and those with special gifts, he would definitely want someone like Gage. Well too bad, he was Elliot's. He was super curious as to what the other special one in Shaye's family was.

Gage shifted back, a look of uncertainty in his eyes. "What did you think?"

"I think you're amazing," Elliot replied, leaning in to press a quick kiss to Gage's lips. He wanted his mate to know that he accepted him, and the beaming smile that took over Gage's face made him want to give more kisses.

"So, you're a griffin. I assume you can fly then too? What kind of gifts come with that?" Elliot knew that some paranormals had special abilities outside of their species' normal ones and was curious as to what his mate's was.

"I can fly. We'll have to figure out how I can take you one day. I have some magic; it's strongest in creating wards, but I can also use it as a tracking signal if I come in contact with someone I want to later follow. I'm immortal, and I can also recognize others like me. Not griffins, I'm the only one, but other rare immortals, the one-offs. TruthSpeak powers also don't work on me. I can feel when it's being used, but I don't feel the compulsion to tell them the truth," Gage said.

"And no one in the Convocation knows you're a griffin?"

Gage shook his head. "My brother is a gargoyle, so we let them assume we were from the same Flight when we joined. Most of them don't even know we're brothers. It's not common to need to shift in front of them, so it's never come up. I took a stationary post, in part because I felt the need to be here, but also because it meant less contact with them in general. Marco is a traveling Warden, so he checks into head-quarters frequently to get his assignments and give updates on his work. There's a higher chance someone would know his species since he's around them more. Because he's a gargoyle and they have the limited immortality, it's always been assumed that his injuries have healed because of that. They don't know about my true immortality and that I shared it with him."

Gage led them back upstairs to sit where it was more comfortable. He might need to figure out a seat for the base-ment for Elliot. Right now, no one else came down and there wasn't a place to sit except on the stairs. He wanted his mate to be comfortable if he ever joined him.

"Okay. I guess it's my turn," Elliot said. "I was found abandoned by my adoptive parents. They never had much luck finding my birth parents. My aunt is a Seer and she has had several visions about me, which is why I'm here in town and also why I was never turned. My mother was never able to have children of her own, so she was a bit overprotective. My family all live in one city, not quite as tight as some of the witches' neighborhoods, but not too spread out either. They kept me safe in the only way they knew how, by keeping me close to home and being overprotective," Elliot said to Gage. He smiled as he felt Gage's leg move closer, pressing gently against him in support.

"I've loved being here, on my own. Well, I still have Shaye and I'm staying at her house, but without my family smothering me. I think the best part is the bakery, I love working there. Bill and Mary are great and I've learned a lot from them when it comes to dealing with having a storefront bakery, not just mail orders like I had been doing. When they retire, I would like to buy it from them."

"So you want to stay here?" Gage asked. Elliot could hear the hope in his voice.

"Yes. This feels like home. Of course, my family is going to want to meet you. Whether that means they come here, or we go visit them, whichever is better with your work," Elliot replied. Between the Warden and the Sheriff positions, he wasn't sure how flexible Gage's schedule would be. But that was another good thing about being here; he had Shaye's whole family to hang out with if Gage was working and he was lonely.

"Would you want to live at the Clan house?" Gage asked, keeping his face purposely bland. He didn't want to sway Elliot one way or the other. He just wanted him to be happy.

"I like it there, but I love your house. Plus, it's closer to your work. Would it be a problem if we stayed here?"

Gage shook his head. "Rolf is a really laid-back Clan leader. He just wants his family to be happy. Gawain even plans on taking road trips and being gone for months at a time when he comes across a dig project he's interested in." Gage personally thought that Gawain had not looked into any digs lately because of Barry.

"How dangerous is the Barry situation?" Elliot asked. He knew he was safe in town, but he didn't want his mate to go into danger and not be able to help. If he stayed human, even with immortality, he would be significantly weaker than any paranormal.

"Pretty dangerous. We've managed to track it back to his father, who seems to have started this whole debacle. They've been taking paranormals for hundreds of years. We still haven't found where they're keeping them, the main base as it were. We've found a few temporary ones, some old and abandoned, but some still in use.

"His father seemed to have forced breeding, trying to either keep a species alive or make a new one or find a rare paranormal. We're not entirely sure. Barry is paying paranormals to mate with ones he assigns to them, if it results in an offspring that is unique or has special powers, he comes back later to take them as part of the agreement. These are the smaller camps we've been finding that are still in use.

"That's what happened to Jimmy. When Marge was kidnapped by Barry in an attempt to access the paranormal library, he had Jimmy using his TruthSpeaker powers. When we discovered his parents had willingly given him, sold him, to Barry, we made it so that Marge and Duncan could adopt him. He's a great kid and he's thriving here.

"Once he discovered we were looking for the camps, he started destroying others. We haven't found anyone else alive after that first one. If there were any kids, their bodies weren't left behind like the adults," Gage said.

"You said he took the ones who were special. Not that all kids aren't special, but what happened to the kids who were more normal, a regular type of paranormal?" Elliot asked. He wasn't sure he wanted to know, but he needed to know what they were going up against.

"We don't know." Gage sighed heavily. "The first camp we found, they refused to tell us. We haven't found anyone else alive to ask. That first one had a registry of sorts, and some names were marked off. Some were children, some were adults. We just don't know what that means: if he killed them, if he released them."

"So I would be safer if I became a paranormal?" Elliot asked.

"I'll keep you safe, so will the town wards. If you want to stay human, I understand. You'll still get my immortality if we mate, and if you join the Clan/Tribe you will get the telepathic link to them as well," Gage said. He wanted Elliot to make the decision best for him, not the one Gage thought was best. Which would be of course to change to a paranormal so he would have extra strength to protect himself.

"Hm. I have the ability to sense magic," he told Gage. "It doesn't seem to matter what kind. I was able to sense the wards on the town, your house, Rolf's house, the Sheriff's station. If someone is creating a spell, I can tell. I could even tell that the pendants everyone was wearing were magicked. What would happen to that if I became a paranormal?"

Gage was stunned. He hadn't heard of anyone with that type of power. He knew Berkley could sense magic to an extent, but not if it was a cloaking magic. To always be able to sense magic was a very unique gift, one that Barry and his group would love to capitalize on. He needed to make sure they never got near his mate.

"Does Shaye know about your gift?"

"I've told her I can sense magic, but I don't think to what extent."

Gage nodded. "I'm not positive what impact it would have. I know Shaye said her gift became more manageable, more stable and not as draining on her. Maybe yours would increase somehow, maybe it wouldn't change anything. I'm not really sure. I've never heard of a gift going away or disappearing after becoming a paranormal though."

"So my options right now would be vampire or werewolf? Maybe jaguar?" Elliot asked.

"Yes. I'm not entirely sure if all cats can change someone or not. Most of them can, but I've never asked her if she had that ability," Gage replied.

"Which one would you recommend?"

"That would be entirely up to you, mate. I don't mind biting, which all of those can do. You know about vampires, since you've lived with them for so long. Werewolves don't need the moon to change. The only thing a full moon does is make them a little more…energetic. And hungry. Some have a slight silver allergy, and of course wolfsbane is bad. But it's a poison, so it's not good for most people. Jaguars, from what she's told me, are more of a solitary shifter. She's getting used to being part of a family, but her own mother left when she was deemed old enough to take care of herself. No allergies or special diets," Gage told him.

Elliot nodded. He had always wanted to be a vampire to fit in with his family, but now he had options. He also wasn't a big fan of blood, which would potentially make it a little more difficult when it came to drinking if he chose that route. Wolves were cool looking, and it's not like he wore a lot of jewelry where it would make a difference if he did develop an allergy to silver. Being hornier once a month didn't seem all that bad. If Gage's friend could adapt from being a solitary person to being involved in the Nightwood Clan family, then he could too. He rather liked the idea of being a cat to match his mate's cat side. Of course, that would entirely depend on if Gage's friend would be willing to change him.

"I always thought vampire, but only because of my family. I don't really like blood," he told Gage. "If I got to pick, I think I would like to be a cat, so we would kind of match," he said, his cheeks turning red. It sounded like a stupid reason when he said it out loud.

"I would like that too, but I'd be happy with whatever you chose. Even staying human," Gage told him earnestly.

"I think I would like to change. It will give me more protection if things hit the fan with Barry. Or even if we go on a trip somewhere, it gives me a little more protection in durability and strength. I think it would make both of us feel better," Elliot reasoned.

"It would for me, but I don't want to pressure you into anything you might regret," Gage said.

"I know you have more experience and skills in protecting yourself, but if it ever came up, I'd like to be better equipped to help you or protect you too."

"The guys at the Nightwood Clan are good at teaching that kind of thing. They taught Shaye, and I think Tess, before the fight with Vlad."

"What fight?" Elliot asked.

10

"Shaye! Where are you? You've got some explaining to do!" Elliot yelled as he entered the house.

Gage followed behind him, bemused. He had thought that Shaye would have told Elliot about Vlad in the week or so since he'd been in town, but then again, she was working at the clinic and helping out at the Paranormal History Museum and Elliot had started working at the bakery.

Rolf came out of his office, an eyebrow raised.

'Everything okay?' he asked telepathically.

'Yeah. Shaye forgot to mention the whole Vlad fight, it seems,' Gage responded.

'Oh. God, that seems so long ago with everything else happening. I can't believe it's only been a year since she saved me the first time. That's crazy. We still don't have a wedding date set either. Maybe after this Barry crap is finished. If we make it a destination wedding, would you be able to come? Ian put the idea of Scotland in my head, and it's stuck there. I'll pay for everyone,' Rolf offered.

'We'd love to,' Gage replied, touched that he would be included.

"What? What's wrong?" Shaye came running out of the library, socks sliding on the floor in her rush.

"You stabbed someone!" Elliot shouted at her.

"What?" Shaye looked around, confused, her eyes settling on her mate.

"Vlad," Rolf said simply.

"Oh. Yeah. But he was a really bad guy," she said. "I forgot you didn't know. Come in and I'll tell you about it." She walked back into the library, Elliot following and asking questions.

Gage shook his head.

"Want a drink?" Rolf offered with a smile.

"Yes. Please. I didn't know getting a mate would cause so many emotions in one day." He was exhausted. The stress he had been carrying since learning he had a mate yesterday had disappeared when Elliot had accepted him, but it left him feeling tired. Of course, he hadn't slept much yesterday either.

"I remember those first couple of days," Rolf commiserated. "The fear they won't accept you, the fear they'll accept being your mate but not turn. How did the talk go?" He handed Gage a glass and they sat in the living room.

"Good, I think. He seemed to accept being my mate and talked about becoming a paranormal."

"Any of us would be more than happy to turn or change him," Rolf offered. "You guys are family."

"Thanks. I think he's leaning toward jaguar, if Marge can and is willing. He wanted to have our animals kind of match. Jaguar to my lion," Gage admitted, not able to stop the smile or the color flooding his cheeks.

"That's sweet," Rolf said. "I'm pretty sure jaguars are one of the cats that can change someone. Marge and her family are coming over for dinner, if you wanted to get the question out of the way. I don't know how that works outside of mates. Does he change first and then mate bond, or vice versa?" Of course, his mother had been changed by someone not her mate, but he wasn't sure what the best way to go about it when it voluntarily involved one person and a mate bond, and another person who would initiate a change.

"I don't know," Gage said slowly, trying to remember if he had met anyone with similar circumstances. Most paranormals changed their mates, if possible, but that wasn't an option for them.

Gawain popped his head in. "Either way. Sorry, I didn't mean to eavesdrop, but I was in the kitchen. I have heard it's easier to do the mate bond first, that way you have a telepathic link in place already if they get scared or the change/turn takes a while."

Rolf nodded. "I can see that. Shaye and I did the mate bond first, the turning came later. Hers took a long four days, but I could at least sense she was fine over the bond. Without that, I think I would have gone nuts. The stress would have been a lot worse. It's up to you guys and what you're most comfortable with, but if I had to do it again, I would still do the mate bond first."

"I'll talk it over with him, and ask Marge tonight." Gage could see Rolf's point. He and his animal would both rest easier if they could sense Elliot while he went through the change.

Elliot followed Shaye into the library. Any other time, he would love to explore it to find a good book and curl up in one of the comfy chairs.

"Since when are you a fighter?" he demanded.

"I'm not. Did I never tell you the whole story of how I met Rolf?"

Elliot shook his head. He had a feeling he might need to sit for this story and sat on the loveseat, Shaye taking a seat across from him in one of the chairs.

"Huh, okay. I got a travel nurse job at the hospital here. I was exploring the town and I felt this overwhelming pain. This is back when I was human, so all my normal problems with empathy and healing. I followed it to a big house, this house, and I heard a voice in my head asking me to 'save him.' When I got inside, I found Rolf chained, beaten. A man was standing there, but instead of attacking me, he disappeared through the window. Rolf was in horrible shape. I was exhausted and I knew he was trying to hide something. His mental guards were weaker with his injuries and I pushed, looking for what he was trying to keep from me. I didn't want to miss healing anything. Well, it wasn't a broken bone; I found out he was a vampire. I passed out; I had pushed myself way too far and was almost dying myself. He gave me some of his blood, just enough that I would recover on my own. When I woke up, he explained mates and paranormals. I know people would say it was fast, but I could feel he was telling the truth. I've always wanted a family of my own, who I could love and would love me in return. So I decided to become his mate.

"I waited on turning though; I was afraid of how it would affect my gifts. Tess came to visit and discovered Sam was her mate. Vlad snuck poisoned blood into the house and Rolf almost died again. Vlad had used one of his minions who worked at the hospital to tamper with the blood supply for Rolf. After that, Rolf was determined to bring the fight to Vlad instead of always being on the defensive. Tess and Berkley created the wards and a battle plan was created. I turned so that I could help and wouldn't be as vulnerable. Ian came to fight with us and discovered Berkley was his mate. They all helped train me so I could help in the fight. We had a safety area set up where the wards would keep Vlad and his people out. It was a group effort and eventually Vlad was killed. His body was burned to make sure he couldn't come back.

"That was early November. Tess and Sam went to visit her

family after Thanksgiving, in the beginning of December. Some of Vlad's minions attacked them, trying to take over Vlad's spot. Tess had thrown a protective spell over Sam, which is the only thing that saved him when he was hit with a death spell."

Elliot looked over as the library doors opened and the rest of the family came in.

"To save Sam, we all took a blood oath to Rolf. It was the only way to circumvent the spell. It had been worded to repel witch magic. Sam was dying, but Shaye was able to share what she saw over the telepathic link, which allowed us to save him," Doc said, as he sat, Emma perching on the arm of the chair he was in.

"Gage told you about his animal?" Doc asked.

Elliot nodded, wondering why they had all come in. He was happy when Gage sat next to him; when an arm lightly wrapped around his shoulders, he smiled and leaned against the huge body next to him.

"Guess it's my turn then," Doc said with a smile. "I'm the other rare paranormal in the group. I'm an alicorn. Gage had sent me the ritual to share my immortality with my family. Of course, I didn't know it was him at the time. We're both members of an extremely secret forum for rare paranormals on the dark web. Turns out, Gage was the creator of the forum and helped share information for all of us. When we saved Sam, my beast thought it meant it was part of the ritual to create his Tribe."

"We already had the Clan bonds, so adding the Tribe bonds didnae seem like a big deal," Ian said. "Then Doc told us about the immortality. That one threw me for a loop. I didnae like drinking blood from anyone but my mate."

"But we all agreed and took part, which was a good thing because we were attacked in Scotland. We had been there visiting Ian's family. He was shot in the heart. He would have died without it," Berkley said, holding Ian's hand tight.

"We're a crazy mess of Clan and Tribe bonds and telepathic links, but it works. You just need to be careful not to broadcast to the wrong person."

"Oh, come on! It was one time!" Ian protested.

Elliot was so confused.

Gage leaned over. "It was during sex. He accidently used the new Clan telepathic link instead of the mate one," he whispered.

Elliot snorted. Gods, that would be something Elliot could see himself doing. Poor Ian.

"Anyway," Rolf said, trying to draw attention away from Ian. "We would like to offer you the Clan and Tribe links, if you are interested. Gage said he couldn't because of the Convocation, but you could. Either way, you guys are part of our family."

Berkley walked over and handed Elliot a pendant. "This matches all of ours. It has the NWC monogram for Nightwood Clan and is spelled. They'll glow when danger is nearby, but no one else can see it, other than us. They also conceal paranormal status from human hunters. Too many of us are known to the Convocation, so if we had it spelled to conceal it from everyone and we ran into a Convocation member, it would look suspicious. They protect against evil intentions. It's not perfect, but they help. Doc's for example, also conceals him while flying and will shrink or expand to fit his form. Gage, I made you one too. I know you have a bunch of wards in place, but I didn't notice a concealment spell. This should let you go flying a lot more often," Berkley said, handing Gage his own. "I have one for Marco when he comes next time too, so don't let me forget."

Elliot slipped it over his head, feeling the magic pulsing inside it.

"I heard you might have a question for me?" Marge asked, smiling.

Elliot looked over at Gage, questioningly.

"*Cat,*" Gage mouthed.

"Um. Yes. If you're willing, no pressure at all. But I was thinking of changing, and I would like to be a cat. So we match. I mean not match-match, but we'd both be part cat," Elliot stumbled. He sounded like an idiot, but he was nervous.

"Of course. Gage is my oldest friend. I would love to help his mate," Marge said. "Just let me know when."

"I'm not sure when yet," Elliot replied, looking over at Gage. He hated to put it all on him, but he figured he would know more since he was older.

"Rolf and I were talking earlier. We thought it might be easier if the mate bond is established first. That way we have the telepathic link between us. I'm not sure if the Clan/Tribe bond should be next or changing?" Gage said, looking toward Doc.

"Hm. I'm not entirely sure," Doc admitted. "Based on the shifter aspect, I would think changing first, that way the animal is already there when we form the Clan/Tribe bonds. I don't think it would make a difference if you joined the Clan and then changed, I think your animal would simply be an extension of you and would automatically be linked in. But I'm not positive either. I can do some research and see if I can find anything, but for now my recommendation would be mate bond, change, then Clan/Tribe bonds."

"What's the timeline look like for that? Do we need to wait in between?" Elliot asked. Of course there would be some time since it wasn't like Marge was going to be standing there while they mated and then bite him, but he wasn't sure if he had to wait long after changing.

"I would recommend at least a few days to a week between changing and joining, just so you can get used to your cat and practice being in your new form before you get the added craziness of telepathic bonds to the rest of us," Doc recommended.

"That makes sense." Elliot nodded.

"I'm always open in the evening," Marge told him. "Just let me know when you're ready."

11

G age drummed his fingers against his desk frustrated. He wanted to check up on Elliot, but didn't want to smother him. It had been a couple of days since they had talked to the family about Elliot turning and joining. It had seemed like they were on the same page, but then nothing. He got some texts and they talked, but no other mention of completing their mating. He wished he knew what Elliot was thinking; he didn't want to pressure him into anything, even though he was now popping an erection around anything that smelled like lemons, the scent his brain associated with his mate. He had decided to stay in his office after a close call when one of the deputies was eating a lemon muffin at his desk. The last thing he needed was for his employees to see him like that. He was old enough that he should be able to control it better, he grumbled to himself. And until Elliot, he could, but his body was demanding its mate.

A knock on the door had him looking up from the paperwork. Shaye stood there holding a to-go bag from the brewery and a potted aloe plant.

"Hi," Gage said, not quite sure what was going on.

Shaye shook her head at him, setting the items on his

desk. "I only have a few minutes before the next patient is due, so I'm going to be quick. You need to make the first move," she told him.

"What?"

"With Elliot. You're going to have to make the first move to push things along," she explained.

"I don't want to push him into something he doesn't want. It seemed like we were on the same page when I showed him my animal side, but after our talk at the Clan house, there's been no other mention of it," Gage said.

"He's waiting on you. You're going to need to take charge in this. His family was very overprotective, so while he's had a few dates, I don't think they went very far," Shaye said, her cheeks turning pink.

Oh. So Elliot might be…huh. That was not what Gage was expecting.

"I know he wants to mate with you, but I don't think he knows how to move it forward," Shaye said. "He lights up when he gets a text or a call from you. Don't forget, he knows how fast paranormal matings can go."

Gage cleared his throat. "I don't have the greatest experience either. I never had long relationships, I believe the modern term is hookups. It was too risky with my shifter side." What a thing to admit, but he wanted the best chance to have a successful relationship with Elliot. If that meant being embarrassed and asking for advice from Elliot's friend, who happened to be a member of Gage's adopted family, so be it.

"I have his favorite lunch in the bag, so take it over and ask if he has time to eat lunch with you. If he's too busy, that's okay, just leave it there and invite him over for dinner. Invite him over to dinner either way. You guys need time alone, so make sure it's dinner at your house, not at a restaurant. Bring the aloe plant with you to lunch. He's not really a flower guy, but he loves potted plants. He used to always have an aloe in the kitchen in case he got burned, but I don't remember seeing it when he moved some of his stuff in," Shaye told him.

"What do I do after dinner?" Gage asked.

Shaye's face turned bright red. "Um. I'll leave that up to your imagination," she teased.

Gage smacked his head down against the desk. Good lord, that's not what he meant, but that was funny, he thought as he snorted.

"Not what I meant," he said, finally letting the laughter out.

"Talk to him again," Shaye said after she laughed with him. "I really don't want to pressure either one of you, and I'm just the messenger for this. Emma recommended it be soon. She and Tess don't have a definite time frame, but he plays an important role in something. When it's cold. Their best guess was end of November, early December."

"Why does shit always happen then?" Gage muttered. Last year's events were still fresh in everyone's minds.

Shaye shrugged. "I don't know. That's all they gave me to pass on." Her phone beeped in her pocket. "That's my alarm. I have to get back to work. You'll do fine. I think you guys are perfect for each other. Good luck," she said, coming around the desk to give him a quick hug.

Gage quickly returned the hug, feeling her push calming vibes at him. "Thanks," he said, grateful he had someone who could give him advice. Marge was his oldest friend, but both of them had been loners. His brother wasn't any better than he was in terms of relationships, and neither one of them knew their fathers, so it wasn't like they could use their parents as an example either. He waited until Shaye left and ran to the bathroom to check himself out. He needed a haircut soon, he thought, but otherwise he looked okay. No coffee stains or eye boogers.

Grabbing the food and the plant, Gage walked out to the

reception area. "I'm taking lunch out of the office. I'll have the radio and my phone if you need me," he told Doris.

"Have a good one," she replied, looking up from her crossword puzzle. "Sean's out on patrol."

"Thanks for letting me know," Gage said as he left.

Walking down to the bakery, he realized he felt nervous. He wasn't used to the feeling. He had been in countless fights, had hidden his brother for years as he scraped by for food to feed them, had arrested many humans and paranormals. None of that compared to facing his mate and hoping he hadn't changed his mind about them.

The bell over the door chimed as he pushed it open. The smell of baking bread and sugar wafted out from the kitchen.

"Be right there!" Elliot called out.

Gage smiled, reminded of the first time he had met his mate a few days ago.

"Oh! Hi," Elliot said as he came through the door. "I was thinking about you," he said, his cheeks flushing.

"Me too. I, uh. I have lunch, if you have time to eat. If not, I can leave it here. And this is for you too," he said, thrusting the plant at Elliot. "And dinner! I wanted to know if you would want to come over to dinner tonight." Smooth, he chided himself. He was lucky Marco wasn't here or he would be laughing his ass off at his blundering.

"Thank you. I would love to come over to dinner. Can I bring anything?" Elliot asked, relieved that Gage was taking control, even if he seemed nervous about it.

"I'm not the best cook. I was thinking spaghetti and meatballs?" Gage replied, inwardly smacking himself for not having come up with a plan for dinner before coming over. He at least knew he had the stuff to make spaghetti at the house.

"I'll bring garlic bread and dessert then," Elliot replied. "I love pasta. Have a seat. I'll grab us some waters for lunch." He placed the aloe plant in the window so it would get plenty of sun. He'd have to see if he had someplace in the kitchen to put it.

As he sat down to enjoy a somewhat awkward lunch with his mate, Elliot couldn't help but hope that this would become a regular occurrence.

Elliot finished helping load the dishwasher, admiring the view as Gage bent over to grab the soap packet from under the sink. The man had a nice ass; not quite a bubble butt, but it had a nice roundness to it. It looked firm, perfect to grab on to. When a throat cleared, his head jerked up to find Gage had turned his head and caught him staring. He hadn't even realized that his hand was already reaching toward Gage. Whoops.

He took a deep breath, letting it out in a loud sigh. "Okay. Full disclosure. I want to be your mate. I'd like to do it tonight, if you want. I've had a couple of first dates, at most some kissing and a little groping. Other than watching porn, I don't really know what I'm doing," Elliot confessed. He thought it was better to warn Gage ahead of time. The man was over two thousand years old. He was bound to have more experience than Elliot and he didn't want to disappoint him.

Gage stood up, tossing the soap packet on the counter before grabbing his hand. "Mate. Look at me," he commanded when Elliot focused on his chest. "I'm not a virgin; I've had…interactions, but I've never had a relationship before. We're both virgins when it comes to that. I haven't lived with anyone in a very long time and I'm still trying to not feel like an imposition or a bother with the Nightwood Clan. We're supposed to be perfect for each other. As long as you can have some patience with me because I'm sure I'll make mistakes along the way, we're going to be amazing. No matter what we do, it will be perfect. I never expected to be gifted a mate, but I'll honor you for the rest of our lives."

"Which will be forever," Elliot said, not quite asking but still looking for confirmation.

"Forever," Gage agreed. He brought one hand to Elliot's face, cupping his cheek.

Elliot's eyes closed as he felt Gage's thumb stroke across his skin. He wrapped his arms around Gage's waist, holding on to him. His head tilted back slightly as Gage gently tugged on his hair. Opening his eyes, Elliot saw Gage looking down at him, eyes flashing amber. As Gage slowly lowered his head, Elliot felt the anticipation gather in his stomach, eagerly awaiting the first real kiss from his mate. They had a tame cheek kiss the first time he had come over, but he wanted a passionate one with lots of tongue and wandering hands.

He moaned as he felt Gage's lips press to his, the beard and mustache a sensation he hadn't experienced before. He wondered if he would get beard burn; he couldn't wait to find out. One of his hands grabbed Gage's head, pulling him even closer. Elliot opened his mouth when Gage's tongue gently licked at the seam. His hips arched, pressing against Gage as the kiss deepened, their tongues rasping against each other. A groan left his mouth as his cock rubbed against Gage's through their pants. He felt huge, even through the fabric. Elliot vaguely wondered if it would even fit. He hadn't taken anything larger than a slim dildo in the past.

Elliot's knees went weak as Gage's large hand slowly traced down his back, following the path down between his cheeks, tapping over his hole. He grabbed on to Gage to keep from collapsing on the floor.

"Let's go to the bedroom, mate," Gage said. As soon as Elliot nodded, Gage easily picked him up, the muscles in his arms flexing. Yum. Elliot wrapped his legs around Gage's waist to hold on. And to rub his cock more firmly against his mate's hard stomach.

As they entered the bedroom, Elliot looked around. A large Californian King bed dominated the room. There was an upholstered bench at the end, a pair of gym shoes underneath. The room was painted in a dark navy blue with light gray curtains, the furniture looked like a cherry or mahogany, and the bed was surrounded by a wrought iron frame, covered in light gray bedding. It looked comfortable. There was a light gray leather wingback chair in the corner, a small table and lamp next to it, a book lying on the table. It was remarkably clean.

"If you don't like anything, we can change it," Gage said, tossing Elliot on the bed and crawling up after him.

"I like it," Elliot said. Really, it would be the kitchen where he would make changes if anything. As long as there was a comfy couch somewhere and a stocked kitchen, he was happy.

Gage leaned over him, unbuttoning his shirt and then unbuckling his pants. Elliot gasped as Gage's knuckles brushed across his dick. He caught Gage's smirk, and ran his fingers through his hair, pulling Gage down. Once his tongue was busy exploring, Elliot pulled at Gage's shirt, untucking it and sliding his hands underneath, exploring his mate's body. Gage's skin was warm, his skin smooth, although Elliot could feel a few raised bits like scars. He especially loved the mounds of muscle on his abdomen, the six-pack just as fun to trace as he had anticipated. Feeling daring, he unbuttoned the pants, sliding his hand in to cup the mammoth there. He wasn't a stranger to porn, but Gage would easily be one of the biggest he had ever seen. He slowly stroked up and down, learning the feel and texture of his partner's cock. Gage was uncut, thick and long. Elliot really wanted a taste, and he brought his hand to his mouth, licking the precum off.

He grinned as Gage let out a small groan. He shrieked in

surprise as Gage suddenly stood up to rip Elliot's pants all the way off. It quickly turned into a moan as Gage swallowed him whole. Elliot wasn't as large as Gage, but he was a decent size, and his mate was having no problems swallowing him down to the base. Elliot could feel Gage's throat contract around him and within an embarrassingly short number of head bobs, his balls drew up tight.

"Gage," he tried to warn his lover.

Gage sucked harder, his finger lightly tracing around Elliot's balls, down to his hole and tapping it lightly. Elliot shouted as he felt his orgasm rush through him. He watched through heavy-lidded eyes as Gage crawled up his body, licking his lips. Elliot could taste himself on Gage's tongue as he kissed him.

"Hmm, we're just getting started, mate," Gage told him, grabbing a bottle of lube from somewhere. As Elliot relaxed into the kiss, he heard the snick of the bottle opening, and seconds later felt a slick finger rubbing his entrance. He automatically clenched, but Gage shifted to cup his balls, giving his dick a few strokes to wake it back up. As his body relaxed again, the finger slowly pressed its way inside. Gage was gentle, slowly thrusting until Elliot was used to the invasion. The second finger burned a little bit, but Elliot knew from playing with toys that he would stretch. He would need to in order to take Gage.

"Oh god," he whimpered as Gage found his prostate. God, he had never found it on his own. His body writhed on the bed as Gage played with him, stroking his fingers over the spot, leaning down to take Elliot's shaft into his mouth again. Elliot spread his legs wide, wanting to feel even more as Gage slid a third finger into his hole.

"Please. Please. Now. I need you. I don't want to come again without you in me," Elliot pleaded.

Gage gave his cock one last lick, moving to kneel between Elliot's legs. He placed a pillow under Elliot's butt, helping to tilt him to the right angle. He pressed Elliot's legs up toward his chest, spreading them as far as they would comfortably go. Elliot took a deep breath and bore down as he felt Gage slowly enter him. Gage was huge, he felt like he was being split in two. Elliot panted as Gage was finally seated all the way inside him. Through eyes hazy with pain and lust, Elliot watched as Gage spat on his hand, moving to stroke Elliot's penis which had lost some of its firmness from the sting of being stretched so wide.

"I've got you mate, relax. We can take as much time as you need," Gage reassured him, holding completely still other than his hands stroking his dick and balls. Elliot had no idea how long it took, but he felt his body slowly adjust to being impaled. As his dick became fully erect again, he gripped Gage's arms.

"Now, move, please," he said.

Gage looked at his face, searching for any discomfort before slowly drawing his hips back. The glide back in was just as slow, the heat from his shaft dragging along Elliot's passage. Gage moved his hands to Elliot's hips, holding him tight and tilting his hips just the tiniest bit. On the next thrust in, Elliot saw stars as Gage hit his prostate.

"Yes, there. Do it again," he demanded, clutching at Gage's back, his heels digging in to keep him tight against him.

Gage leaned down, pressing his lips against Elliot's, their tongues twining together, the rasp of their tongues mimicking the rasp of their bodies sliding against each other.

"More," he muttered against Gage's lips. "Fuck me and claim me."

Gage reared back, his eyes fully amber. Elliot thought he would have bruises from how hard Gage was now gripping his hips, but he didn't care. All that mattered was the love and wildness in Gage's eyes as he let loose and absolutely pounded into Elliot's ass, hitting his prostate on every stroke.

Elliot grabbed his own dick, stroking it, knowing his orgasm was almost there.

He tilted his neck to the side, letting Gage have access to claim him. He wailed as Gage thrust deep, filling him with his cum, the heat of it startling.

"I take you, Elliot, as my Mate. To love and cherish forevermore," Gage grunted out, striking out and slashing his shifted hand against Elliot's shoulder.

"I take you, Gage, as my Mate. To love and cherish forevermore," Elliot repeated. As he felt the bond form between them, something urged Elliot to mark his mate, causing him to dig his nails into Gage's skin, leaving bleeding wounds against his hip.

Gage collapsed over top of him, catching himself on his elbows so he didn't crush Elliot. "Are you okay? Was I too rough?" he asked, not wanting to leave his mate's body quite yet, but wanting to make sure he wasn't causing him any pain. He would need to get some salve on the mate marks soon, at least until Elliot could visit Shaye and get them healed.

"Hmm," Elliot hummed, pulling Gage closer. "It was perfect," he said, kissing Gage gently on the lips. "I could nap though," he admitted.

Gage held Elliot tight, rolling them to lie on their sides. He kept them connected, not letting his dick fall out just yet as he pulled a blanket over them. He grabbed his shirt and quickly wiped the cooling semen off Elliot's stomach. He watched and listened as his man's breathing slowed and his face relaxed completely in sleep. Gage sent a quick flare of magic out, checking to make sure his mate was alright and the house was secure. When all was well, he let his eyes close, following Elliot into sleep.

12

Elliot woke, groaning at how sore his body was. He might need to start stretching before sex. He wasn't used to those positions. He grinned though; it was everything he had hoped it would be. He could feel the mate bond and he reveled in the sensation of being connected to another person so closely.

'Morning,' Gage said, pressing a kiss to his shoulder.

'Morning,' Elliot replied, grinning like an idiot, he was sure. The telepathy was so cool.

"That was quite the groan. Are you okay?" Gage asked, trailing a hand lightly down Elliot's back. He loved seeing the contrast between Elliot's pale skin and his darker tones. "Was I too rough?" He lost some of his control right at the end and went a little harder than he was planning for his mate's first time.

"No, it was perfect. Just not used to being bent into that shape." Elliot smiled. "I'm going to start daily stretching," he joked.

"Or we try different positions," Gage said, moving from a caress to gently massaging Elliot's hips and legs.

"Hmm, that feels good," Elliot moaned, relaxing into the

bed. He drifted for a while, allowing the sensation of his muscles loosening to pull him back toward sleep. He felt a kiss to his back before Gage pulled away and covered him with a blanket.

"Stay here. I'm going to get some coffee started and get a bath going for you. I have some Epsom salts I can add, they should help your muscles."

Elliot lay in the soft cocoon, sensing the deep contentment coming off of Gage. He would need to call his family later to let them know he had accepted his mate. He also wanted to talk to Gage again and see if he could bring his family into the Convocation matter. Elliot was positive that his family could help. If nothing else, they could lend support if another fight came to the family. He had no idea how much time passed, but Gage came back into the room, gently pulling the blankets off him and picking Elliot up. As Gage carried him into the bathroom, he took a deep breath, letting the scent of his mate surround him.

He let out a sigh as he was lowered into the water. It was the perfect temperature and smelled faintly like lavender. There was a travel mug of coffee sitting on the ledge for him.

"Thank you," he said, pressing a kiss to Gage's hand. "This feels wonderful."

"I'm glad." Gage smiled at him. "Do you have work today?"

"I'm supposed to stop in for a meeting with Mary and Bill this afternoon. I think they want to go over plans for Christmas. I know they want to travel to see their grandbaby for the holiday."

"Are you going to be able to handle the bakery all by yourself? It gets crazy busy from what I remember. I can help on my days off. I'm not a baker, but I could help at the front," Gage offered. He really was not good at baking, hence why he was at the bakery so often. He had a feeling that Elliot had no idea what he was getting into during the holiday season. It started picking up in October when people wanted cute Halloween things, then from a week or so before Thanksgiving on was a mad house. He had seen lines wrapped around the block. There was no way a single person could handle all of that. The town did a big Christmas market that also drew in the tourists.

"I would love your help. Does it really get that busy?" Elliot asked, a hint of nerves in his voice.

Gage nodded, taking a seat on the floor next to the tub. "The town does a great Christmas market and it brings in a lot of people, plus the regular orders from people in town and a few neighboring towns. Bill and Mary are known locally for having great products."

"No pressure," Elliot muttered, dropping lower in the water.

"Hey now," Gage protested. "Everyone loves your stuff. I can feel your doubts and they're bullshit. You're an amazing baker, just as good, if not better than Mary. Don't tell her I said that though."

Elliot smiled up at him, receiving a gentle kiss on the lips. "Thank you. I will definitely take your help. Maybe I could hire someone for the season. I'll ask them when I go in today. If I can get someone to work the front of the house, I could focus on the baking."

"Elliot! Thanks for coming in today. I won't keep you long, I just wanted to talk to you about the upcoming holiday season. We were hoping to go visit our daughter and granddaughter for a month and wanted to make sure that would be alright with you," Mary said as she gestured him to sit.

"You should totally see your grandbaby at Christmas. It's so much fun watching them open presents," he encouraged her. He remembered having a blast watching his cousins' kids at Christmas. They were always so excited.

"We get extremely busy here," Mary warned.

"Gage told me. Would it be alright if I hired a seasonal employee to help out while you were gone?" Elliot asked.

"Well, that's the other thing I wanted to talk to you about," Mary said with a smile. "Bill! Get out here and grab that envelope for Elliot."

Bill came out. He had a smile on his face, so Elliot wasn't too worried. Bill was pretty easy to read most of the time.

"We're giving it a month to live down there to see how we like it," Mary said. "But we're thinking of making it a more permanent move. All of our kids moved away and besides the bakery and some friends, there's nothing keeping us here anymore. We love the town, but we'd like to be closer to our kids at this point."

"Oh, wow. I didn't think it would be that soon. I can understand wanting to be by your family though," Elliot replied.

"Here," Bill said, handing over the legal-sized envelope.

Opening it, Elliot saw a few sheets of paper and a hand-written note. He pulled the note out first.

"We will always love you and want you to visit whenever you can, but that town is your home, where you're supposed to be. Promise. Love you always, Mom and Dad. PS. When things have settled, we expect you to bring him home to meet everyone."

Well that didn't help clear anything up, he thought. He pulled out the rest of the paperwork, realizing that it was legal documents and the deed to the store.

"What the—" he shouted, stopping himself before he cursed in front of Mary. The deed was in his name.

"I haven't even gone to the bank yet to get the loan. How is this possible?" he asked, confused, hopeful, and did he mention confused?

"Your parents called on one of your days off to see how you were settling in. No, no, don't be embarrassed," she urged when Elliot groaned and dropped his head to the table. "They were so nice and as a mom, I can understand wanting to know how your child is doing. They arranged to buy the bakery in your name, as a surprise. They didn't want you worrying about a loan.

"We'll still help out until we leave, make sure you get your off days. It'll give us time to say goodbye to everyone, although we'll come back for visits. But it also gives us time to make sure you're set up to run it, point out any quirks in the equipment that you might not have come across yet. That kind of thing," Mary said with a smile. "This way, you can start making any changes you want and getting your own bank account for the business set up before we're gone."

Elliot nodded, still flabbergasted that his parents bought him a bakery.

'Are you okay?' Gage suddenly asked along their bond. 'You had a surge in emotions, but I can't figure it all out. Do you need me to come over?'

'No, no, I'm fine. I'm just...shocked? My parents apparently had been talking to Mary and Bill and bought the bakery for me. It's mine. What am I going to do with a bakery?' he asked, suddenly panicked that he would ruin everything Mary and Bill had built.

'Same things you have been doing. Making amazing baked goods, setting the prices, selling goods. You've been slowly taking over and I don't think you've even realized it. You run the money to the bank, order the supplies. I think Mary's been easing you into running it all on your own. You're going to do great. And if you need help, you have me and the whole Nightwood Clan behind you. There are several business owners in the group, if you need help with that kind of stuff. Taste testers for new products. Heck, I'm guessing they'll even help work in the store, if you need them to,' Gage pointed out.

'Thank you. I panicked for a minute. You're right. I can do this,'

Elliot replied, thinking if he said it enough he would believe it himself. This was everything he had ever wanted. He sent a wave of love to Gage before turning his attention back to Mary.

"This is incredible. Thank you so much," he said sincerely, getting up to wrap her in a hug. She had been an amazing mentor so far.

"You can always call or text us if you have any questions once we're gone," she offered. "But I know you're going to do great. Now go on and get out of here. The papers have already been filed, so it's all legal. Go enjoy the rest of your day," she urged.

Elliot gave them both hugs and thanked them again for trusting him with their bakery. He was in a bit of a daze as he walked into the Nightwood Clan home. Luckily everyone else was at work. He made his way to his room and plopped down on his bed. Pulling out his phone, he took a deep breath before he called his mother.

13

G age pulled out his phone to send his brother a text message. He knew he was busy with the Barry case, even more than Gage had been so far. As a traveling Warden, Marco got pulled in on more cases. With his stationed position, Gage's responsibility was to his town and district. At times he was pulled away to help on a case, but at least for this one he was able to stay here most of the time and utilize a lot of online and book research. He really needed to check in with Gawain this week and compare notes.

The wait was starting to wear on everyone, he thought. Ian had cancelled a Renaissance festival that he had been planning on attending. He hadn't wanted to risk bringing problems to a human-run event on the chance that Barry was looking to attack any of the Nightwood Clan members. There hadn't been any obvious threats, but Tom had warned them that Brandon had been receiving a few concerning texts and emails. When they tried to trace the messages back, they ended up being burner accounts. Nothing was explicitly said, but there were enough "bring one to me" type of messages that they were all on heightened alert. There was also certain wording that made it clear he was talking about the Night-wood Clan and their town. Unfortunately, there was nothing concrete that they could arrest Brandon for. It had been all vaguely worded directions and threats.

Gage had never been more grateful that the town was warded. It was almost Halloween and it meant that they could all enjoy the holiday without worrying about Barry coming after them. This would be Jimmy's first Halloween since he had been taken from his home two years ago. He was planning to walk around with his friend Dave and a couple other classmates. Gage would be driving slowly through the town, handing out candy and making sure the older kids and grown-ups didn't cause any trouble. For the most part, the town was pretty well-behaved, but every couple of years someone tried to stir things up.

Elliot said he was going to hand out pumpkin-shaped sugar cookies at the bakery and had a few non-food items for the kids with allergies. After trick-or-treating was over, they would be going back to the house for a birthday party for Shaye. Elliot told him he was thrilled to see that her birthday was finally being celebrated, as her parents had ignored it every year. Elliot had already bought her a present. Gage didn't know what he was going to get her, but if he didn't come up with any great ideas, he knew books would always be welcome.

He was looking forward to the pumpkin carving contest the family was having a few nights before Halloween. They were going to the farm to pick out their pumpkins, although Gage wasn't entirely sure why when the grocery store had them sitting right outside for people to buy. Elliot told him it was all part of the experience. There was a bottle of whiskey up for the prize.

He had already started sketching out his design. He had no idea if he would be able to actually carve the two cupcakes handcuffed together, but he was going to give it his best shot. Normally he only carved a single smiley-faced pumpkin to sit in front of the station for Halloween. Sometimes his deputies carved others and placed them around the office. Elliot was keeping his design pretty quiet, so Gage wasn't sure what he was making.

Gage looked down when his phone vibrated.

MARCO: Another dead end. I feel like one of those dogs chasing their own tail…tired and accomplishing nothing.

GAGE: Why don't you come for Halloween? Take a break. You can hand out candy with the family. We're getting together for Shaye's birthday after. There's the pumpkin carving contest on the 29th too.

Gage waited for a response, watching the three little dots as his brother wrote a reply. He already knew that Rolf had invited Marco but thought that he might need that extra little push to accept the invitation. Now that Gage had Elliot, he was over at the house more often and he was getting used to the notion that he could just show up. He knew that Marco suffered from the same hesitance to intrude, even though they knew they were welcome, and didn't have a mate to drag him over there all the time.

He finally stopped waiting for Marco to respond. Based on the amount of time it was taking, he was probably deleting and rewriting his message over and over.

"Stop being a dork and come. I have to beat you at the pumpkin carving contest," Gage said as soon as his brother answered the phone.

Marco laughed. "I've seen the pumpkins you've done in the past. I'm not worried. Do you…are you sure…"

"They've adopted us," Gage said softly. "They consider us family and I know it's hard to adjust to having one besides just the two of us again. You mentioned moving here, so you better get used to getting invited, or dragged, to a bunch of events," he lightly teased. It wasn't even that many things, Sunday family dinner and game night, the occasional birthday or grill-out, and holidays. There were other things of course, but they were good about inviting and not pushing.

He heard his brother sigh on the other end of the line. "Fine. Be prepared to lose to my awesome carving skills," Marco finally said.

"Right," Gage scoffed. "I'll see you then. Be safe."

"You too." Marco hung up.

Hopefully he would show up. Although Marco was good about keeping his word. Gage made a mental note to try to draw him in more often. They had gotten so used to their routines. With the ease of texting and their telepathic link, they were bad about getting together often in person.

His griffin was still restless, a sure sign that something was coming. Sometimes it took months, but his gut hadn't been wrong yet. Gage pulled out his tablet. This one had so many security features and wards on it, it took a while to log on. It was only used for one thing though. When his forum finally came up, he looked through the recent activity, trying to do a safety check for his people. Well, they weren't really his. Most were people he had only met once in passing, but they were all rare paranormals. But because he was older than any of them and he had created this forum, he felt responsible for them in a way.

Anonymous1: *Safety check-in. Please reply to let us know you're safe. There has been an increase in hunter (both human and paranormal varieties) activity. I'm not sure if you've heard, but there was a Convocation member involved. Some are still being investigated and the leader is on the run. He has been kidnapping rare gifts and species, so please be careful. If you hear/see something suspicious, please reach out. I know some of the people investigating, ones I would trust with my life, and I'll pass the information on.*

He hit send and set an alarm to make sure to check the forum later in the day. Some of the members only logged on once a month, so he could only hope that most of them saw the message. Leaning back in his chair, he switched over to his work computer and scrolled through his emails. Other than the Barry investigation, it was pretty quiet. He was debating whether to do a walk around town when his phone chimed again.

ROLF: Can you come over after work today? Gawain has something he uncovered during his research.

GAGE: Sure. I get off at dinnertime today. Need me to bring anything?

ROLF: Nope. Dinner's in the slow cookers. Can you let Elliot and Marco know?

GAGE: Will do. See you then.

He wondered what that could be about. Gawain had been looking into historic paranormal disappearances but had been a little tight-lipped about what he was working on. He liked to make sure he had his facts right before he shared too much information.

"Do you know what this is about?" Elliot asked as they walked up the driveway.

Gage shook his head. "Rolf didn't say, just that it was something Gawain had uncovered. I know he was looking into past paranormal disappearances trying to find any connections to Barry."

Elliot used his key and unlocked the front door. They could smell the beef stew from here and it smelled amazing. Elliot's stomach growled, reminding him that he hadn't eaten since breakfast, other than a quick muffin for lunch.

Merri stuck her head around the library door. "Grab some food and come on in. Gawain has a whole presentation ready," she said, rolling her eyes. The affection was there for everyone to see though.

As they settled onto one of the couches, Gage noticed that Jimmy was working on his computer with headphones on.

"He's working on his math homework while listening to music," Marge said as she walked over to them. "Any idea of when you might want to initiate the change?"

Elliot looked at Gage who shrugged.

'*Up to you,*' Gage said. It was Elliot's choice and his body that would change, not his. While he wanted Elliot hardier, he would love him either way.

"Can we wait until after Halloween? I think the first few days of November would work best, right before the busy season but I don't want to do it at Halloween time either," Elliot replied. Thanksgiving and Christmas would be horrible to try to fit that in. He had a feeling his senses would be stronger and wanted to give himself time to adjust before the holiday madness happened. He also knew about Emma's and Tess's predictions, so he wanted to be ready by then.

"Sure. I would recommend staying here so someone is nearby as you adjust. It only takes a day to really take hold, unlike vampires who can take up to four days, but sounds and smells may be different, and you'll want to practice changing and moving in your cat form. The woods here are perfect for that. Would the second work? You should be finished and able to attend Sunday dinner the next day. Your cat would be able to get the scents of everyone then," Marge added.

Elliot nodded. "Sounds good. Thank you." He would talk to Rolf and Doc and set up joining the Clan/Tribe that next weekend. That should be before it got cold, hopefully. He had actually meant to do this all sooner, but with the bakery and getting to know Gage, it had fallen to the wayside.

"Okay. Everyone eat, and I'll present," Gawain said.

Elliot looked at Gawain. He was almost vibrating with

excitement. He didn't know him that well, as Gawain had been holed away doing research for most of Elliot's time in the house, but the man looked almost giddy. He pulled out a large map that had little sticky arrows scattered around it, setting it in the middle of the large table.

"With all the kidnappings, I decided to look into more disappearances, see if any of them could be linked to Barry or his father. I figured that if we could narrow down when they started, we might be able to also narrow down the area. Traveling back in the day was a lot harder and it would make sense for them to focus on a certain area to begin with. There's always the possibility of them doing that, but then later dragging everyone to their main building that we're searching for. At this point, I figured any data could help point to a pattern.

"I found some cases here and there, which I passed on to Marco and Gage. The one I've been hunting for though, that one took more time and I finally figured it out. I tracked down some of the family of the village and finally convinced them I was a good guy they could trust, at least a little bit. They told me stories of their ancestors and I think it fits. The village was a mix of humans and paranormals, but it seemed like they were like we are here, that the humans knew about it. When people began disappearing, they contacted their neighboring friends for help. Eventually the survivors left before any more of them went missing. Because they didn't want to draw the attention of anyone wishing them harm, they kept a low profile. They left a message for anyone who would come looking for them, but they also put spells in place to keep people away from their new home." Gawain beamed at them.

Elliot was so lost. Was that supposed to have made sense? Looking around the room, he saw the others looking just as confused.

"Gawain, honey. I think you missed a part," Merri gently reminded her mate.

"What?"

"The village. No one knows what you're talking about," she told him.

"Oh! Right. Roanoke. It was Roanoke."

14

Elliot's ears were ringing with the noise in the library. A loud whistle split through the air, silencing everyone.

"Warn me next time," he muttered to Gage, wincing. He would have covered that ear.

"Wait a second. You mean Roanoke, the "Croatoan" carved into the tree and fort Roanoke?" Shaye asked.

"That's the one," Gawain confirmed.

"I had no idea it was a paranormal village," Tess said.

"I didn't either until I really started digging in. We've found evidence that Barry or his dad were active at the time and the story of an entire village disappearing had always caught my attention. Other people had looked into it, even back in the day, so I never really delved deep into it. At first, storms and other things kept them from having any conclusive evidence of what happened. There were no signs of a struggle, which made it odd to me when the theory that they were attacked was put forth. Not that it was impossible, there is evidence that they weren't on the best of terms with some of the locals. But without bodies or signs of a struggle that seemed like a weird theory to have settled on. There were over a hundred people unaccounted for. The Croatoan carved into the wood may have been a note that they left to go to Croatoan island where they got along with the native people. There is even some evidence to support it now based on a recent archeology dig. As everyone knows, White checked out the island when he finally made it back but he didn't find them. However, if they were running from something, I'm guessing that they would have spelled the area to keep people from finding them. After all, someone had been kidnapping them."

Gage was flabbergasted. He was alive during that time, although not really near there, but still he had no idea they had been such a large group of paranormals.

"So all one hundred plus settlers moved into Croatoan island?" he asked.

Gawain shook his head. "I don't think so. I think they split up. While there is the saying 'safety in numbers,' it also made them sitting ducks for whoever was preying on them."

"And you think it was Barry or his father?" Rolf asked.

"Yes. The humans, sure they could have been killed by enemies nearby, but the paranormals should have been able to defend themselves. Unless it was against another paranormal. If it was Barry's father and he had the ability to paralyze like we believe, it would have made them an easy target. I don't know how many he could affect at once or for how long. Obviously, Roanoke wasn't in the dessert, so he would need to move them somehow to the location we believe Barry is still using."

"Okay, so how does this help us now? The site's been studied, at least by human archeologists and nothing else pointed to where they might have gone. Could they hae left a paranormal type of message?" Ian asked.

"I have Rob reaching out to his contacts to see if anyone has worked on the sites or noticed something. He loves weird things like this, so it's not really going to throw any red flags that he's asking. I know it's not realistic to think that they left a detailed description of any strangers near their village, but if we find the main location, some of them may very well still be alive and could testify against Barry. Even if it was his father who took them, Barry would have been there to check up on his collection and didn't release them for all this time."

"That's true. Some of the older ones would have seen Barry bringing in new people and could testify to that," Gage added. They had enough evidence to arrest Barry now, but having witnesses testify would certainly help get him convicted.

"Gage, I'm also running records checks on properties. It's geared toward large land properties that have stayed with a single owner or family since at least 1580, since that was around when Roanoke was established. Now, there wouldn't have been records then, but they must have gotten a deed at some point. There is no way they would risk someone laying claim to their land. The search is aimed at magically altered deeds. We all know it can be done, and there's an entire database of them. I don't know how much it will narrow it down, but I'm focusing it first on out west and then the rest of the United States. Places like Daryl's ranch will potentially show up, so we'll have to weed through them, but it's a start. Rob has Daryl and Rick asking around to their friends and families as well. Ranchers talk to each other, so maybe someone will know of a landowner who doesn't quite fit in."

"I didn't know you had access to those files," Gage said, giving Gawain the side-eye. He was certain Gawain didn't have that level of clearance; even though Gawain worked for the Convocation sometimes, it was more as a contractor than a full-fledged employee.

"I don't," he replied cheerfully. "Marco got me backdoor access. With the Brandon thing, I didn't want to trust the Convocation to run the search. They should be doing it themselves, but if they have more tainted people, it might not get done or the results could be buried."

Gage nodded. It made sense, although he hated breaking the rules, he needed to keep his family safe.

Emma got up and left the room, coming back a few minutes later with a tray. Yum, brownies. There was a large coffee station in the corner that also dispensed hot water for the tea drinkers. "Grab some dessert. I've already been snacking on it all day and need it gone," she laughed, making sure she brought one over to Jimmy first. The brownie was perfect, fudgy and chocolatey but the edges were crispy. Elliot never could make a perfect brownie and he started to get a tickling of an idea. He knew Emma suffered from anxiety though and wasn't sure if the bakery would be the best place for her.

'I think she might like it,' Gage told him, nudging his knee against Elliot's. Clearly he had been thinking loudly.

'I don't want her to feel pressured to say yes and then have it set her back. You've all said how much better she's been,' Elliot said. Tess and Shaye were also good bakers, but they had other jobs. Elliot would need help over the holidays for sure. It could be a test run, but that was like throwing someone in the deep end to teach them to swim.

'I think she would tell you no if she thought it was too much. Doc definitely would. We can set up a safe room of sorts in the back, additional wards, something to make her feel safe there. If she did a lot of work in the back, or at least had that opportunity, I think it would be a good fit.'

'Maybe after I change and join the Clan/Tribe. I can get used to my new senses, she can get used to being in the bakery and I can train her on the cash register. I could really use the help, but I don't want her to feel like she has to and then be uncomfortable,' Elliot said.

'You could always bring it up now, let her come visit or hang out at the bakery, get a feel for it so she can make a decision. Then

after you join, she can come in for training if she's interested,' Gage replied.

Elliot nodded. That made sense. He wondered if he had enough money to hire another part-time person, someone who could help with the front of the store when it was busy so he could stay in the back and bake. That was his favorite part. If he baked a lot early in the morning, maybe he'd have enough done that he could work the front and let Emma retreat to the back of the store if it got too busy. A second person on the cash register would be helpful though; that way someone could box or bag up the baked goods while the other person rang up the order. Maybe he could bring it up before he left tonight; either way, he needed to make some decisions quickly on hiring someone.

"Was there any other ground-breaking, history-changing things you wanted to tell us?" Sam asked around a mouthful of brownie.

Gawain laughed as he reached for his own piece. "That's it for the day. I think they settled in a few different spots, including with the Croatoan island peoples, and used concealment spells to stay hidden."

"There have to be some of their ancestors left. Why wouldn't they come forward after all this time to let historians know what happened to the colonists?" Tess asked.

"If I'm right, and they were paranormals, they couldn't very well tell a human that they were hiding from another paranormal and that they used a spell to stay hidden. Plus, if the story was passed down through the family, maybe they're still keeping themselves hidden. Maybe not with a concealment spell, but definitely by not revealing that they're related to the Roanoke colonists. Now, it does make me wonder about the archeologist who found the evidence that they had moved over to Croatoan island. There is a mix of European and native artifacts there, but still no final clue about what happened to them. It would make sense that they would have kept things really secretive after being preyed on by another paranormal."

"Are you thinking that he's a descendant? Or another paranormal? Or a curious human?" Shaye asked.

"Or do ye think he works for Barry? Trying to hunt down any loose ends?" Ian asked.

Gawain shook his head. "I don't think Barry has enough time right now to care about something that happened so long ago. If they were already written off, he wouldn't bother. I think it's more likely that he's either another paranormal historian who was curious like me or a descendant. I've got an email out to him to try to set up a time to talk. My name is recognizable in both worlds, so it should lend enough credence to my request that he may talk to me. And if he is a descendant, then he may talk to the other families and realize I'm on their side of this thing and be more willing to speak with me. I spoke to a couple, but there's bound to be a lot more out there."

"What are you hoping to find out if you talk to him?" Gage asked.

"Several things, starting with if he's human or paranormal. Why he is interested, why he performed a dig there, and if he's paranormal, I'm going to work my way into asking about why they left. See if I can't find out if my theory about Barry or his dad being involved is correct. If they were involved, if I could get any copies of documents from the colonists that may have survived, write down any stories that were passed down through the generations, any speculation the remaining colonists had about what happened. I heard a few stories, but I know there must be more. If there are descendants, they may still be in touch with each other and if he is a descendant and trusts me, he may be able to encourage the others to share more with me. There had to be something special about the ones taken, although I'd imagine they would keep that information pretty quiet," Gawain replied.

"Do you think he'll get back to you?" Shaye asked.

"Maybe. I'm known for being interested in weird and quirky digs, so it shouldn't look too odd that I'm reaching out if anyone is paying attention. If he is a paranormal, then he may have heard I'm part of the Nightwood Clan. And as the lovely," Gawain said with a lot of sarcasm on the word, "Convocation member mentioned when she barged in, we're getting a reputation. If he's heard that we're inclusive and that the town is warded, he may be curious enough to respond. The fact that we've been involved in looking for the hunters and Barry would also be in our favor. All of it indicates that we're going to be on his side and can be trusted," Gawain added.

Rolf nodded slowly. "If he wants to meet, maybe it would be good to try to get him to come here. The risk would be if Barry or someone working with him was watching for visitors, but at least our wards would guarantee that he didn't mean us any harm. If you absolutely have to go to him, I would prefer that you take someone else with you, maybe Marco if he's available. He could get you out of a situation quickly if there was a problem. I just don't want you unprotected outside the wards while Barry and the hunters are still active."

Gawain gave Rolf a look. "I can take care of myself, but I know what you mean. I would probably tell any of you the same thing," he sighed.

"I can't say for sure, but Marco may be able to pick up the archeologist and bring him here. That way it decreases the risk. Although of course maybe it would bring greater attention to him. I'm not sure what the best answer is. Marco could bypass the driving or flying part of the trip, but having Marco transport him here may bring its own unwanted attention if someone is watching town and suddenly spots a new visitor that appeared out of nowhere."

"What if Marco brought him directly to the house? None

of the wards will let them enter if he means us harm. Barry's people wouldn't see him if he stayed inside. Marco could transport him back home the same way," Berkley suggested.

"That could work, if he would agree to stay inside the house," Gawain mused. "I'll bring up the options if he contacts me and is willing to meet."

15

"Remember, no magic but you can use any other tool to create your design. Place your finished pumpkin on the front porch. When all of the designs are done, cast your vote in the jar. You have two hours, starting now!" Tess said, clicking the timer start button.

Gage had to laugh as everyone rushed to grab their pumpkin and supplies and headed off to their own spot to work. Marco had in fact made it for the contest, and he was so pleased his brother was getting a break from the stress of his job.

Elliot was sitting close but was turned enough away that Gage couldn't see the design he was tracing onto the pumpkin. Gage carefully traced his design, making sure not to smear the ink before it dried. As he cut the lid off and scooped out the guts, Shaye ran two bowls over to them.

"Not looking! Here take these. One's for seeds, one for the stringy and cut out parts," she said, her head turned away as she held out the bowls.

"Oo! Are you making pumpkin seeds?" Elliot asked excitedly.

"Yup! As soon as I'm done with my pumpkin, I'll collect the seeds and roast some," she said.

"Can you make extra? We can send some home with Marco, and I'll snack on them through the week," Elliot asked.

"Sure!" she agreed before hurrying off to work on her pumpkin.

"Pumpkin seeds?" Gage asked, a little confused. He'd had them in muffins and in granola or trail mix, but not by themselves.

"Yup. Roasted with a little oil and salt. They're good, nice and crunchy. She makes them every year if she carves a pumpkin," Elliot replied.

"Huh," Gage said. He had never had them like that, but it sounded good. He focused on the small cuts he needed for the handcuff links.

'I'm going to beat you,' Marco crowed in his head.

'We'll see,' Gage replied.

The two hours passed much too quickly and Gage only had part of the details done that he wanted to get in. Maybe he should have practiced first. The main design was there, but he had wanted to thin out parts of the cupcake bases to create lines for the wrapper. He thought it still got the concept across.

When he placed his pumpkin on the porch, he saw all the other offerings and realized that there was no way he was winning. There was a stack of books with a tiny dragon curled up on top, a wolf howling at the moon, an anvil with a hand holding a hammer about to strike a piece of metal, a cat riding a dragon. Each one was impressive and he smiled as he saw Jimmy put his carefully on the porch. He had made a traditional jack-o'-lantern face.

As they sat around the fire on the back patio, they munched on snacks and the pumpkin seeds and enjoyed some of the brewery's fall specialty drinks, including a non-alcoholic cider for Jimmy. Gage grabbed another handful of the seeds, wrapping an arm around his mate as they laughed with their family.

Elliot pulled the last of the cookies out of the oven, looking at the clock. He only hoped that they cooled fast enough that he could get them iced and bagged up before the trick-or-treaters came. He had a small cake boxed up and ready in the refrigerator for the party tonight. The bell dinged from the front door.

"Be there in a minute!" he shouted. Maybe he should get a camera pointed at the door and a TV to see the feed in the back room. It would at least let him know how quickly he needed to scurry out to the front. If it was family, they would give him a bit more time than a customer would.

He looked up as a throat cleared softly in the doorway between the kitchen and the cash register area.

"Emma! What are you doing here?" he asked, surprised to see her there. "Not that you're not welcome. Are you okay? Anything wrong?" Elliot rambled, not wanting her to feel like he was being rude. She just normally didn't come in by herself.

Luckily, she laughed at him. "I'm fine. I know everyone is busy tonight with the trick-or-treaters. Gawain and Merri are at the museum, Sam at the brewery, Ian and Berkley at the Winged Potter, Gage on patrol, Marge and Duncan at the library, Shaye and Rolf at the house, Albert's at the clinic. You didn't have anyone here to help, so I thought I would stop by and see if I could help," she offered with a smile.

"Oh! That's very nice of you! You aren't hanging out with Doc?" he asked.

"Tess is there now. I had a question for you, too, so I'm not being completely altruistic with my offer," Emma said, sounding a little nervous.

"Sure, what is it?" he asked, sliding the last tray on the cooling rack and walking them to the freezer.

"Um…I know you're here by yourself a lot. Bill and Mary are leaving to see their granddaughter, which is completely understandable," she added hurriedly. "But the lines at Thanksgiving and Christmas can go for blocks, and then there's the Christmas market if you wanted to have a stall there as well. Bill and Mary used to, but I wasn't sure what your plans were," she said.

Elliot nodded, not quite sure where this was leading.

"I may not be the best, but I am a decent baker and cook. I'm working on the whole peopling thing. But I was wondering if you needed help?" she asked in a rush.

Elliot was taken aback. He had seriously thought she would turn him down when he was going to ask her, but instead she came to him.

"You won't hurt my feelings either way," she assured him, probably taking his silence the wrong way.

"I was just talking to Gage about this! I was going to ask you," he said. "Seriously, I was going to see if you were interested after I changed. I meant to do it earlier, but I underestimated how many Halloween baked good requests would be coming in. I was trying to think of a way we could make it comfortable for you: in the kitchen area, or only in the front when it was slow. I would love it if you worked here; I never could get my brownies as good as yours and I think those would be a great addition to the shop."

Emma smiled at him, excitement and relief in her eyes. "After Jimmy went to school, I realized how bored I was," she laughed. "I help Albert with his filing once a week and check in on the farm in England. But there's only so much knitting I can do. I'd like to give it a try, if you're willing. I think maybe working the front when it's slow would be a good start, and I can always help in the kitchen if you need me."

"Why don't you grab an apron and you can help me ice

the pumpkin cookies? I fell behind today and I'm hoping I can get them done in time for the trick-or-treaters," he told her. He was excited. Emma was such a nice person and she did make delicious baked goods, so he thought it would work well for both of them. He would keep an eye on her and make sure it didn't become too overwhelming. He needed the help, but not at the expense of her mental health.

"Do you have the icing already made?" Emma asked, tying the apron on around her waist.

"Shoot," Elliot muttered. "No. I forgot that. I'll get that made right now."

Emma nodded. "Are these the bags? I'll get them laid out with the ribbons so we can bag quickly."

"Thanks. It should only take me a few minutes to get it ready. I'm doing royal icing. I was thinking the outline in a darker orange, the flood icing in a little lighter color, and then a green for a stem and a leaf. If we don't have time, we can just do the stem and leave the leaf off, I think."

He got to work making the icings to the right thickness and color. He watched as Emma used a clean counter to lay out the bags, a ribbon to tie them above each bag.

As he filled the piping bags with the icing, Emma came back to help. Pulling the cookies out of the freezer, he was happy to see they had cooled enough to ice. Handing a tray to Emma, taking another one for himself, they got to work on decorating the little pumpkins. He thought they would turn out cute and the kids would like them. He also had a bin of non-food items under the counter to grab for the allergy kids. No one wanted to be left out on such a fun night.

There was a companionable feel working with Emma, the silence not uncomfortable, and he got into his groove pretty quickly. Pretty soon they had finished the cookies, and he placed them near a fan to help them dry faster. Together they cleaned the kitchen and the front seating area. Emma helped him with some last-minute Halloween decorations and getting the lights set up.

"Thank you for your help," he told her as they began packing up the cookies. The kids would be coming around soon. Elliot remembered always trying to leave a few minutes before trick-or-treating started so they would have more time. He'd imagine the kids here were probably the same.

Elliot knew they were eating at the party but that was still a couple hours away, and he was feeling peckish. He probably had enough muffins for tomorrow morning to spare some so he and Emma could grab a quick snack. As he went to pull open the storage door, the front doorbell chimed and seconds later his mate was peeking into the kitchen.

"I thought you were getting ready to drive around?" Elliot asked, smiling at the sight of his guy. They had talked earlier in the day, but they both had a busy afternoon, and he wasn't expecting to see Gage until after trick-or-treating.

"I am, but I wanted to see you and I knew you were going to be busy and probably wouldn't stop to eat lunch," Gage replied.

Elliot felt his cheeks heating. Gage already knew him pretty well. He shook his head, not really having an excuse other than there was a lot of work to do. He couldn't stop the smile that came over his face when Gage pulled a bag from the brewery out from behind his back.

"It's not much, just a sandwich and some fries to hold you over," Gage said bringing it closer.

Elliot reached up, pulling that handsome face down to his. "Thank you," he said before pressing his lips to Gage's.

He heard a light thump as Gage blindly dropped the bag on the counter. Two large hands pulled him closer, his body now flush against his mate's. Gage took control of the kiss, his tongue plunging into Elliot's mouth. Elliot moaned softly at the taste of his lover.

A quiet giggle reminded Elliot that they weren't alone. Good thing or he would have climbed Gage.

"Oh! Sorry. If I knew you were here, Emma, I would have brought two," Gage apologized, his cheeks red. "Do you want me to run and get you something?"

Emma shook her head, still smiling.

"I'll share. We can split it and add in a breakfast muffin. That was my plan before you showed up," Elliot offered.

"I better get going," Gage said. "I'll see you tonight." He pressed a quick kiss to Elliot's lips and gave Emma a nod goodbye.

Elliot looked over when Emma cleared her throat. "Am I going to have that to look forward to?" she asked.

"Uh…" he wasn't sure how to respond. He thought she was teasing him, but he didn't know her very well yet to be able to know for certain.

"Don't worry. That was hot," she told him.

Elliot could feel his face heating up. "Okay," he said. It was pretty hot, he thought to himself with a grin.

"I'm just teasing," Emma said, laying a hand on his arm, looking at him in concern.

"I know. I won't say anything when Doc stops over," Elliot teased back. "Now let's eat. I'm starving."

Elliot looked around as they finished eating, making sure everything was good to go. He wanted to leave as soon as trick-or-treating was over. The kitchen was cleaned up, napkins refilled, the cash for the day in the safe in the tiny office. He'd run it over to the bank tomorrow at lunch if he could, otherwise he'd drop it off on his way home tomorrow. Seeing the first signs of kids coming down the street, he ran over to move two chairs to sit outside. He grabbed the folding table and threw his spider web tablecloth over the top of it and placed the cookie basket and non-food items on it. He closed the bakery's door behind them, leaving it unlocked so he and Emma could still get inside, but making it clear that he wasn't open for regular business right now. Normally he would be closed, but he wanted to be here for the trick-or-treaters. They were adorable in their costumes and he could remember how excited he had been when he was a kid. He wanted to continue the tradition Bill and Mary had started by giving away goodies for trick-or-treating.

The rest of the night was spent handing out cookies to the steady stream of kids. As it got closer to eight o'clock, the end of trick-or-treating, Elliot started handing out the cookies to the adults as well. He already had a cake for tonight's party, and he didn't think many people would buy pumpkin cookies tomorrow. He could make them again for Thanksgiving maybe. They seemed to be a big hit and were easy enough to do.

Shutting off the lights, he locked the door behind them.

"Ready to go party?" he asked Emma.

They walked down the street to the Clan home, seeing the pumpkins still lit, their designs all in a row. He was glad they had their own traditions. It had been a lot of fun having the pumpkin contest and he couldn't wait to celebrate Shaye's birthday tonight.

The dinner was delicious as always and Elliot's cake went over well. He had made a layered cheesecake and cake combo with Shaye's favorite flavors. She seemed happy with her birthday dinner, even if her cheeks glowed bright red as everyone sang to her.

16

"Are you ready for this?" Gage asked, concerned. "We can always do it another day."

Elliot gave him a look of disbelief. "No. It has to be today. The weather forecast is predicting a cold front coming in, and Emma, Tess, and my aunt have told me something is going to happen when it's cold. I want to be ready.

"I just need to tell her today. I've been putting it off. If she finds out after, she'll kill me," Elliot told him.

Taking a deep breath, he hit the green button to finish making the call go through. Seconds later a face appeared on the screen.

"Hey, Mom," Elliot said, trying to smile for her.

"What's wrong? And don't tell me nothing. Your face looks like you haven't pooped in a week," she said, leaning closer to the screen and squinting as if that would let her see him better.

Elliot groaned while Gage bit his lip to keep from laughing. He had forgotten what mommas could be like. Emma was like a mom to everyone, but she used a gentler approach.

"Mom!" Elliot protested. "Nothing's wrong. I just wanted you to meet my mate."

"Did you finally find your sac and seduce him?" a male voice called out from off-screen.

"Shut up, Baz!" Elliot shouted, his face bright red.

Baz was the cousin that Elliot was the closest to, if Gage remembered correctly. They sounded more like brothers. He was going to bite through his lip at this point, he thought as a small snort escaped. Elliot glared at him.

'Sorry,' Gage apologized.

"Ellen! Get in here," his mother shouted, calling for his aunt.

"I'm right here. Geez. I think the neighbors heard you," his aunt teased as she walked through the doorway.

"You are the neighbor," Elliot pointed out.

"So I am," she replied with a grin.

"Well, where's your mate?" Baz asked as he crowded in behind them.

Elliot looked over at Gage, beckoning him closer. He hadn't been far, just far enough to be out of camera range when the call started. Gage sat next to him, taking hold of his hand. Elliot loved all the little touches Gage gave him throughout the day. Sometimes it was holding hands, sometimes a hug, or Elliot's favorite, a kiss to the head or a light hand grazing his cheek.

"Everyone, this is my mate, Gage. He's the Sheriff here, as well as the local Warden. Gage, this is my mother, my aunt Ellen, and my cousin Baz. Where's Dad?"

"He got called over to the mayor's office. There have been a couple of teens who have gone missing and they wanted to see if your dad could pick up the scent trace and see if maybe they were just at another friend's house, if they stopped at the bus stop. Something that would help track them down."

"My dad has a very sensitive nose, more so than most shifters," Elliot explained. "If they run into a dead end or the police dogs aren't successful, they'll call in my dad. The mayor is a paranormal."

'Is missing people common? Do you think it could have some-thing to do with Barry?' Gage asked. It was a bit of a trek for Barry from the last point anyone had seen him, but he was probably on the move a lot.

'No, it's not common. We have a good amount of paranormals in town, similar to here. Most of them are good people and keep an eye out on their neighbors, both human and paranormal. The crime rate is really low. It's not too big of a city, but it's not small either, so there are plenty of things for teenagers to do,' Elliot mused.

"Make them stop," Baz whined. "They're doing that mate telepathy thing."

Elliot looked back to the screen to see his cousin wink at him. Baz was sometimes a bit much, but Elliot loved him.

"I have a few things to tell you, but I'm going to keep it short right now so I can get to the really important stuff," Elliot said, making sure he was making eye contact with them. "First, I'm mated, but still human for now. Second, the bakery is wonderful and amazing. Emma is my first employee and we're getting along really well. She's like the mom to everyone. I think you'll enjoy getting to know her, Mom. Third, I'm changing tonight. To a jaguar. There's a reason I picked that and not vampire, but I'll have to explain that in person later. Fourth, I need someone to come down here as quickly as possible."

"A cat!" Baz shouted incredulously. "I did not see that one coming. I'll head down with Rog tonight. Between the two of us driving, we should be there in a day or two. We'll grab a room at the bed and breakfast. What do you need from me?" he asked seriously.

"Can you grab a few more of my things? Mostly clothes, especially cold-weather ones? Once things settle here, we'll come up and stay for a few days and meet everyone and I'll finish packing up then."

"Make sure you grab his hiking boots," his aunt said, her face concerned. He could tell that she knew something was going on. "I'm sending a note for you," she said. "I think in person is better to talk about this, but the note will have to do for now."

"I was thinking Uncle could come over and help make things quiet for when Baz comes back," Elliot replied, trying to get the point across that there should be a silencing spell without saying it out loud.

"Yes, I agree. I'm going to have him come over right now," his aunt said, pulling out her phone and sending a text.

"What is going on?" his mother asked, looking very confused.

"Sheryl. I'll tell you after Bob gets here. Trust me," his aunt replied, looking straight at his mother, who gave a brief nod in response.

"I'll send Baz back with a letter for everyone. I miss you guys," Elliot said, trying to tell them he would explain what was going on.

"And cookies," Baz interjected.

"And cookies," Elliot agreed, smiling.

A few minutes later he heard a door slamming shut and his uncle ran by with his bag.

"I'm going to go help," his aunt said. "Be safe, nephew. I look forward to your letter and your visit. It was nice to meet you, Gage."

After she left, shutting the door behind her, his mother looked at Baz before looking back at him.

"Are you alright?" she asked quietly.

"I am. I'm happy here. There's just some things that have been happening that we need to be careful about. Baz can tell you when he gets home. You know the thing you were always worried about? You might have been right."

"Oh! You mean the C—" she started, but Baz quickly put his hand over her mouth.

Elliot nodded, not wanting to verbally confirm. "Until Uncle Bob is finished, you need to be careful. We aren't sure how to protect the phone lines, so that will have to wait," Elliot explained.

Baz pointed to himself and Elliot nodded. He knew Baz would pick up on the fact that Elliot would tell him and he would be the messenger to the family.

"I'll go pack up and grab Rog. I can't wait to see your cookies…I mean you," he teased.

"Be safe," Elliot cautioned.

"I'll take the other car," Baz promised.

They talked a few more minutes with the standard getting-to-know-you questions. His aunt came back into the room.

"All set. Sheryl, let's grab some tea and chat. I'm sure the boys have lots of things to do today."

"Love you. Be safe. When you come to visit, your bedroom will always be open," she told Elliot, blowing a kiss at the screen.

"Love you too, Ma," Elliot replied before clicking end on the phone.

"You okay?" Gage asked.

Elliot shrugged, taking a second to gather his thoughts. He hated not being able to tell his family everything, but he understood why the Clan was keeping things quiet. Baz would be here soon and he could tell them then.

"I just wish I didn't have to keep things from them," he said finally.

"I know, but it won't be too much longer I hope," Gage said. He tugged Elliot closer, pulling him to sit in his lap, wrapping his arms around him. They sat like that for a few minutes, Elliot relaxing as he was surrounded by Gage's warmth. Finally, Gage pressed a kiss to his head. "You ready to head over to the Clan home?"

Elliot took a deep breath and nodded. Marge and the others had tried to walk them through it, but the other shifters had been born that way. Shaye was the most recent one in the house who had been bitten, but she was a vampire so it wouldn't be quite the same. Marge had offered to introduce him to Steve, but he had been turned by his mate. Elliot didn't feel comfortable talking about it with someone he didn't know, so they would muddle through it together.

Gage locked up his house and opened the car door for him. Elliot gave his mate a smile; he didn't want Gage to think that he didn't really want this, but he was worried about the future. What was coming that was so important that he needed to be changed by the time it got cold?

It only took them minutes to pull into the driveway. As they walked into the house, he saw a "Happy Change Day" banner and could smell baking bread and beef stew.

"Hey guys!" Shaye said as she rushed forward to give Elliot a hug. "You okay? You seem stressed."

"Just got off the phone with Mom. I hate not being able to tell her everything, but Baz is coming down in the next day or so to bring information back to them. Uncle already put a silencing spell over the house," Elliot replied as he could feel her calming his nerves.

"Come on, let's eat," she urged, pushing them into the kitchen where there were loaves of still warm bread, stew, and a large sheet cake on the counter. He knew it wasn't one of his, it looked like it came from the grocery store. Why wouldn't they have used one of his? Maybe it was supposed to be a surprise, he thought as he walked over to see it.

Elliot burst out laughing as he read the top of the cake. "'It's Not Bestiality If You're Both Shifters.' Who did this?"

Sam couldn't stop laughing as he raised his hand. Elliot shook his head, but he was still laughing. It made some of the stress fall away and he was less worried about what the event was. It didn't have to be so solemn. He was completely relaxed by the time they finished dinner and it was time to head upstairs.

As he, Gage, and Marge left to go to their room, Tess gave

him a hug. "Don't worry, Elliot. It's going to go purfectly." She grinned as everyone else groaned.

He laughed, returning the hug. "I forgot how much you love puns," he said.

"I'll have to use them more often then!" Tess said excitedly. "I can't believe you forgot."

"Call if you need me. I'm taking the day off tomorrow so I can be here," Shaye said, giving him a hug.

As they got to their room, Elliot went into the bathroom to take care of business and change into loose boxers. The plan had been to have Gage take them off as soon as Marge left and cover him with a sheet. That way they wouldn't get ripped or tangled when he changed, but he wouldn't be naked in front of Marge. As much as he was used to paranormals, his family were vampires and he was not as comfortable getting naked around other people as shifters were. He would need to figure that out, as most shifters needed to get naked in order to change.

"Okay, Elliot. Sit on the bed and I'll bite your other shoulder, not the one with the mate mark. You should fall asleep pretty quickly. I'll leave so Gage can get you settled, but I'll come back in to keep an eye on you and to help coax your cat out if needed. Just like we talked about already. Any questions?" Marge asked.

Elliot shook his head, pressing a kiss to Gage and gripping his hand tightly as he sat. He tilted his head, giving Marge room.

There was a sharp pain as she bit down, and he felt something racing through his body. His heart sped up before slowing back down to normal speed. Elliot fought to keep his eyes open as drowsiness pulled him toward sleep. He knew it was normal based on what Marge and the others had told him, but he still fought it. The last thing he saw was Gage's gray eyes.

17

Gage stayed right by Elliot's side. As his eyes finally closed, he lowered him to the bed. Marge touched his shoulder as she stood up.

"I'll grab us some coffee and a snack and I'll be back in a few minutes. My cat is telling me everything is going well," she said.

Gage nodded, keeping an ear on Elliot's breathing and heartbeat. As soon as Marge left the room, he pulled Elliot's boxers off and draped a sheet over him. The sheet shouldn't get in the way when he shifted like the boxers would but would still allow him some privacy. Laying a hand on his forehead, he felt a little warm, the change starting to take effect. He pressed a kiss to Elliot's forehead before sitting back.

Marge came back in few minutes later carrying two coffee tumblers and a basket of snacks. When Gage raised an eyebrow in question, she laughed.

"Tess said it would be easier to carry this way. They packed a lot of food in here, so I hope you're hungry. They said if we need more, just call and they'll bring more or come sit with him if we need a break."

"Thanks," he murmured as he took the coffee. He couldn't imagine leaving Elliot's side though.

They sat in silence for a while, listening to the sounds of Elliot's heart and breathing slow down and speed up as the change took effect. They had sent up some of Gage's favorite lemon poppy seed muffins, as well as some of the protein bars Berkley made for Ian. There were pretzels, chips, some cookies and fresh fruit as well. It was a nice variety.

"How is the search going? Has Marco had any luck?" Marge asked, breaking the silence.

"No," Gage replied, shaking his head. "It's driving us both nuts. There should be a trace somewhere of Barry's family holdings, but we haven't been able to find any yet. I know it exists, but I think it must be an off-grid type of place. There are no other bills or accounts linked to him for utilities, so for it to have water or power, it must be self-contained. If it is out west like we think, solar would probably be a good option for power, maybe wind. Water could be scarce, but maybe they had a well or he gets it shipped in. Marco's looking into large water deliveries while Gawain is still trying to weed through the large ranches and landowners.

"Unfortunately, we don't have a lot to narrow down the area yet, other than where the dessert willow grows. That took it down to a handful of states, but it seems like it's still a lot to sort through. Nothing Barry has done has been legal so far and I'm wondering if he has also spelled the deed or the property in some way so it wouldn't register."

"Aren't most deeds or titles spelled to change names to match the new identities as paranormals grow older?" Marge asked.

"Yes, but those automatically update with the Convocation records. It's a way to make sure we don't get exposed to humans as we age, but don't lose our property either. The Convocation has a whole team that is dedicated to helping paranormals keep their property as they reach ages past a normal human one. There were too many cases where someone left for twenty years or so and came back to find their property had been sold or someone was squatting on it and now had legal claim to it since the landowners hadn't taken any action for several years.

"There are some like Daryl's family, who had one paranormal register it and then made it look like they sold it and it now belongs to a human family since they don't trust people in the Convocation and didn't want them knowing paranormals lived there. The fact that a paranormal was once there would help explain any traces of paranormals or magic that might be felt by anyone passing by. Which has proven to be smart; Barry would have taken them for sure.

"In this case, I'm wondering if Barry went a step further and did an illegal spell so that it wouldn't register in the Convocation database, or if it was never registered and he used a spell to mask the presence of paranormals. He would have had the opportunity and the means to make sure that the property was never officially registered," Gage explained.

"So how do we find it then?" Marge asked.

"Gawain is checking land records, seeing if they stayed under the same name or family. Which most of the long-standing ranches would be kept in the family. But he's also plotting where these ranches are and looking for any gaps between registered properties, BLM land, federal or state parks. If we can find the gaps, we may be able to search those areas that aren't registered to anyone and find it that way. It's got to be easier than just flying over multiple states and hoping we discover something."

"That makes sense," Marge agreed. "Is Marco the only one looking at the properties?"

"There are one or two other Wardens who we know are clean and have the ability to fly, who are checking them out. There are a couple other land-based ones that are investigating properties as we find them. Those take more time, since they can't just roam people's properties until they find something suspicious, in addition to the time it takes them to get there. Once we find any unregistered properties from Gawain's search, we'll send anyone who's close and trustworthy out to search it," Gage replied.

As they finished their coffees, Marge ran the cups back downstairs. Shaye popped in to check on Elliot, seemingly happy with how things were going.

"He looks good," she said softly, resting her hand briefly on Gage's shoulder. He could feel the tension that he wasn't even aware he was carrying fall away. "I'll check on him again in the morning but come get me if you think anything's wrong. Try to get some sleep," she told him.

Marge came back with a blanket and a pillow from her room. "I'm going to grab a quick nap," she said as she curled up in the recliner. "My cat's listening, so I'll wake up when he starts to change."

Gage nodded, waiting until she fell asleep to curl up next to his mate. He could feel the muscles tensing and releasing as the change worked through him. He rested a hand over Elliot's heart, letting the feel of it beating soothe him.

Mine. Okay? His beast asked.

Yes, he's okay, Gage sent back. He had a feeling his beast knew that but wanted the confirmation. They both had been amazed that they had received a mate after all this time. He wouldn't say he fell asleep, but he definitely drifted for a while until he felt Elliot's body stiffen. Marge jumped up, coming over to stand next to him.

"This is it," she said, staring intently down at Elliot. Her nose was twitching as if her cat was scenting the air. "Come on, you can do it," she encouraged softly. She made a soft sound in her throat, the sound distinctly cat.

Elliot's body twitched before he suddenly sprouted fur and his human form disappeared. He was gorgeous. He took after Marge in that he had melanism resulting in the black fur.

Gage hadn't been sure if he would be a regular jaguar or a black jaguar and had forgotten to ask Marge. Of course, she had never changed anyone so maybe she wouldn't have known. Either way he could see it for himself now. His fur was soft, completely black although when Gage looked closer, he could see the jaguar's trademark rosettes. He wondered if Elliot would have kept his blue human eyes or if they changed when in his cat form. Elliot's nose sniffed the air in his sleep, scenting the room. When he caught Gage's scent, he burrowed closer, laying his head on Gage's leg, a contented sound coming from his chest.

"He's good," Marge said, a bit of relief in her voice. "He should wake up in a couple of hours. I'll talk to him, work him through a few things, let him get used to the smells in this room before we venture downstairs and outside. I don't want him to get overwhelmed. Grab some sleep while you can," she told him.

Gage leaned back on the bed, keeping his hand on Elliot. He let himself fall fully asleep now that the change was successful.

18

Elliot's nose twitched. What was that smell? It smelled like a cinnamon roll, heavy on the cinnamon, with cream cheese icing. Yum. He opened his eyes, wondering why the colors were so off. Was he losing his vision? Why was everything blue and green? He tried to sit up and fell off the bed. Trying to stand up, he noticed he didn't have hands and feet anymore, but paws.

Gage leaned over the side of the bed, clearly trying to keep from laughing. "Are you okay?"

Elliot tried to speak, but only a chuffing noise came out. He nodded his head instead. He managed to get his paws under him and stand up enough to sniff Gage. He was what smelled so good and he leaned forward to lick his mate.

"Morning," Gage said, rubbing his head.

"Careful, Elliot. Your tongue's a lot rougher in this form. A couple of licks is okay, but if you lick too much in the same spot, you could draw blood," Marge warned as she came over. "How are you feeling?"

'Good. Vision is weird. I forgot animals are color blind. Not quite used to the paws,' he told Gage, who passed it on.

"You'll get used to it. Don't think too hard when you try

walking. Your brain is going to want to try to walk humanlike since that is what it is used to, but if you don't think too much and let your instincts guide you, you'll do fine," Marge advised him.

Gage climbed out of the bed and stood on the other side of the room. Elliot wanted to pounce on him. He looked so good in the mornings, his eyes a little sleepy. He found himself moving forward and looked down to see his feet. As soon as he paid attention to himself, his feet tangled together and he stumbled. Shaking his head, he kept his focus on Gage, letting the scent of his mate draw him over, trying not to think about what he was doing.

"Good job," Marge cheered as he reached the other side. "Are you ready to try going downstairs and outside?"

Elliot nodded. He knew he was in control, but he was still a little apprehensive about meeting everyone in this form.

As they left the room, he could smell breakfast cooking downstairs and the scent of bacon drawing his feet down the stairs. Entering the kitchen, he found Shaye and his new family there. Taking a deep breath, he could sense each of their unique scents, but they all registered as family to his cat.

"You're gorgeous, Elliot," Shaye said, slowly walking over to him. He headbutted her hand, encouraging her to pet him. She laughed but rubbed behind his ears. "You look perfect health-wise. Go run outside; I'll set some of the bacon aside for you," she promised.

Gage opened the door and Elliot slowly walked outside, the air seeming crisper and more aromatic than he had ever smelled. He could tell there were paranormals and wild animals nearby, as well as the scent of humans from town. He could even distinguish the scent of the cars in the garage. He caught a new scent of cat as Marge joined him on the porch in her jaguar form. She made a chuffing noise, but he had no problem figuring out what she wanted. As she took off running toward the woods, he looked at Gage before following. He knew his mate would run with them. The wind flowed over him, ruffling his fur. It was amazing and he loved it. As he followed Marge up into a tree, he marveled at how easy it was, his claws digging in and letting him climb. She jumped down, leading him to a pond where they took a quick swim. This was so much fun.

After an hour of exploring, she led him back to the house. She nudged him toward the plate of bacon waiting for him and he scarfed it down. He was so hungry.

"Let's go upstairs and get you changed back," Gage said as he towel-dried off any remaining water. "They have more breakfast waiting for you when you're done."

He bounded up the stairs, eager to be human again and talk to the rest of the family. Marge came in a few minutes later in her human form.

"Okay. So this part is kind of up to you," she said. "Each person has their own way of doing it, but you focus on a human thing. For me, it's my human body. For others it might be a scent, something that smells different than when they're changed. It might be how it feels to do something. Don't get frustrated if you don't find it right away; just try different things," she encouraged.

Elliot tried focusing on what he looked like as a human, but that didn't seem to do anything. He tried to remember what his favorite cookie smelled like, but all he could smell was Gage's cinnamon roll scent. Oh! Gage. How it felt to hold Gage's hand, to run his fingers over his hair and across his body, to hold his…

Elliot was suddenly human again and hurried to cup his hands in front of his cock, which had started to get hard envisioning the feel of Gage's skin.

"Alright! Congratulations! You did great. I'm just going to go now. Grab breakfast or something," Marge said, turning around quickly and leaving the room.

"Thank you!" Elliot shouted despite his embarrassment.

Gage eyed him hungrily. "Welcome back, mate," he murmured as he dropped to his knees in front of Elliot.

"Shouldn't we go eat breakfast?" he asked breathlessly.

"In a minute." Gage smirked up at him. "I'm having some now."

Elliot shouted as Gage suddenly engulfed his cock in his mouth, swallowing him down. Oh god, he wasn't going to last long, he thought as he watched his dick slide between Gage's lips. He had the perfect pressure, taking him deep into his throat, his tongue slowly licking back and forth across his shaft. When Gage's hands came up to cup his balls, Elliot lost the battle with himself to make it last and came down Gage's throat. Once his breathing returned to normal, he dropped down to return the favor, reaching for Gage's pants.

Gage grabbed his hand, pulling it up to kiss the palm. "I came when you did," he said. Elliot looked down, noticing a damp spot on the front of his pajama pants.

They jumped into the shower, quickly rinsing themselves off before dressing and heading downstairs. Elliot was startled to realize that even though his eyes returned to his human levels of color observation, he could still smell with his cat's senses.

There was a huge plate of food waiting for each of them and he was amazed at how hungry he was. He ate everything on the plate and even went back for seconds.

'Shifting uses a lot of calories, especially a first shift. The first one also uses a lot of energy. You'll probably be ready to go back to bed soon,' Gage told him telepathically as his mouth was full of pancakes.

'Really? I slept so much yesterday,' he replied, surprised.

Gage nodded. *'It's a lot of work on your body. Not sure why, but after the first time it gets easier. You're still hungry, but the tiredness isn't there for other changes.'*

Elliot shrugged. Well, there were worse things than taking a nap with his sexy man. He grabbed some more bacon. He didn't know if it was his senses or if he was just that hungry, but everything tasted better.

He finally felt full and sat back.

"Damn. And I thought Sam ate a lot on the full moon," Gawain said, staring at him.

Elliot felt his face turn red. He had eaten quite a lot. He had to laugh though as Merri smacked Gawain's arm.

"We'll have to have a bacon eating contest on the next full moon," Sam said eagerly.

"I don't know if that's a good idea. You both might be shifters, but you should still eat fatty foods in moderation. I can't even imagine how much bacon the two of you could go through when your appetites are increased," Doc said.

"We'll still do it," Sam stage-whispered to him.

Elliot nodded. If felt nice to be included and he'd never say no to bacon.

Tess just sighed and refilled her coffee. "We may have to place a special order, or everyone in town will be mad at us for clearing out the bacon section in the grocery store."

Rolf nodded, pulling out his phone. "Do you want regular or thick-cut bacon?" he asked.

Elliot and Sam looked at each other. "Thick cut," they said at the same time.

"If you give yourselves stomachaches, I'm not helping," Shaye threatened. She had a smile though, so Elliot knew she would still help if they ate themselves stupid and felt sick.

"You know who can eat a lot of bacon?" Gage asked. "Marco. He's a bacon fiend."

"Ooo! Yes, let's make it a thing. Ask him to come. Do we know anyone else?" Sam asked eagerly.

"Ian needs lots of calories," Berkley put out there, ignoring the glare from his mate.

"Me? I dinnae eat that much!" Ian protested. "I can give it a shot, I guess."

"Maybe Marshall?" Gage suggested. "I've seen him eat a lot at the brewery."

"Who's Marshall?" Elliot asked. He didn't recognize the name.

"He's the local mechanic. He's a tortoise shifter. He recently found his mate; they both live in Rockfort but had never really met before. Steve, his mate, the one Marge mentioned talking to about being a shifter, was a bit of a homebody. We were all a little shocked when they paired together."

"I'll ask them the next time they come into the library, or if Merri sees them first at the museum," Marge put out there. "I think it would be good for them to make more friends in town. Steve is still getting used to paranormals and it would be good for him to see us in a more normal setting. Not that we're normal," she added, laughing.

"Can I do it too?" Jimmy asked.

"Of course you can," Rolf told him with a smile. "Okay, once we know how many people want to do it, I'll place the bacon order. We'll have to order about a week ahead and will probably be cooking it using all the ovens here."

Elliot wondered when the next full moon was, as his eyes started to get tired again.

19

Elliot was experimenting with a new recipe. He was trying to make a braided seeded loaf of bread. On one hand, his new senses were great because his nose was even better than a timer when it came to knowing when things were close to done, but it was also distracting. He had never noticed just how many scents there were in the world. Even if he couldn't hear them, he could now smell everyone walking past the building. Emma had been helping in the store this week, along with a few of the others. They were working at the front, giving him time to adjust to having these senses without having to be facing all the customers.

The extra telepathic links from joining the Clan and the Tribe had come in handy. He was able to ask for help without disturbing the customers or having them think something was wrong. Good lord, he didn't think he had ever been bitten so much in such a short amount of time. Rolf had bitten near where Marge had when she changed him. He had thought that it would have been weird drinking blood, but when it came to Doc's ritual, his cat didn't seem bothered by it at all. They had done both rituals on the same day.

Although Gage wasn't technically allowed to join, it seemed that some sort of telepathic link had occurred anyway. No one was really sure how it had happened, as he hadn't been involved with the rituals other than standing there. It wasn't as strong as the bonds that had been formed by a bite or by blood, but if Gage concentrated really hard, he could talk telepathically to any of the Nightwood Clan members.

Emma and Rolf seemed to have the easiest time reaching Gage, but they had telepathic gifts to start with. Shaye was able to with a lot of effort, probably due to her empathic gift. The rest couldn't really reach Gage as well; they could project feelings or images, but general speaking didn't seem possible. If Gage reached out first, they could talk, but it was tiring for both sides. Gage seemed happy though; it was more than he had ever expected in terms of getting his own bonds with the family.

Baz was due to come in today. He had been delayed first at home after Uncle Bob put on the silencing spell on his parents' home. His aunt wanted to make sure he was caught up on the issues. Baz wasn't sure if they were being followed, even with using the car that had been spelled against tracking and attacks and had taken some crazy route down. Rog had come with him so at least they had been able to trade off on the driving.

It was just after lunchtime when his nose twitched, his head lifting from where he had been rolling out cookies for the after-school rush. He could have sworn he smelled something that screamed family. He heard Emma's voice from the front of the store talking to someone, but he couldn't make out who it was. Wiping down his hands, he walked to the front.

"Baz! Rog. You guys were supposed to call when you got here," Elliot said, pulling off his apron to give his cousins a hug.

"By the time he remembered, we were already out front," Rog replied dryly. "I was sleeping."

"Sit down, I'll grab you both a snack," Elliot said, moving toward the back.

"Cookies?" Baz asked hopefully.

"Sure," Elliot replied, shaking his head. He had already set some aside for them.

"Did you get checked into your hotel yet?" Elliot asked, moving to sit with them. He looked at Emma as she started to move toward the kitchen. She gave him a small smile and held up her pointer finger. Ah, she needed a minute. She had done great this week, but both his cousins were huge. He nodded back in understanding.

"Not yet. Figured we'd stop and say hi first," Baz said. "Mom filled us in before we left, but we need to get your side."

Elliot nodded. He had a lot to fill them in on, and Gawain had made some copies of documents to send back as well.

Emma spoke to him mentally from the kitchen. *'Rolf said to invite them over to dinner. The house is secure for talking.'*

"Why don't you guys get settled in, explore the town a little bit. If you have time, the Paranormal History Museum is great; I think someone is there today. Come over for dinner tonight and we can talk then. It's just down the street, but I'll text you the address," Elliot said, pulling out his phone to send both the museum's and Rolf's address.

Baz finished his cookies, standing to give Elliot a hug. "I'm glad to see you. Not just for the cookies," he teased. Dropping his voice to a whisper he asked, "Did we scare the lady?"

Elliot shook his head. "Not you, just her past," he replied quietly.

"Ah. Emma?"

Elliot nodded, looking at his cousin questioningly.

"Mom," Baz replied simply.

Just how much had his aunt seen? Elliot was very curious now as to what she had told Baz before they left.

The alert sounded at the gate and Rolf looked at his phone before buzzing the person in. It must be his cousins, Elliot thought looking at the clock. There was a white chicken chili in the slow cookers and corn muffins being pulled out of the oven. The whole family had made it a point to be here tonight, even if it wasn't Sunday. He stayed back, allowing Rolf to let them into the house. Not only was this Rolf's personal house, but it was also the Clan home. While he knew Rolf didn't really stand on ceremony, Elliot had a feeling that he would still want to greet members of another Clan personally at the front door.

Gage took his hand and Elliot couldn't quite read the look on his face. He thought his mate looked a little nervous.

'Are you okay?' he asked, gripping his hand a little tighter.

Gage nodded. *'It just seems different meeting them in person than over the phone.'*

'Is Marco coming tonight?' Elliot asked.

'He was planning to, unless something comes up. I have a feeling that the Baz and Marco combination could be trouble,' Gage said, a smirk in his voice.

Why would he think that? Elliot thought about it for a minute and horror dawned as he realized that those two would definitely play off each other. They were both a little loose with the rules when it came to those they loved. Marco was more subdued at first glance, but when you got to know him, he had a wicked sense of dry humor. Baz was louder, more attention grabbing, which was how he liked it. *'Maybe it's not too late to tell Marco to stay home,'* Elliot said.

Gage felt the air shift and smiled. *'Too late. Marco just got here.'* At least his life wasn't boring anymore.

They had to bring in a folding table for the newcomers but placed it right at the end of the huge dining table. The food and conversations were great as usual and once they helped clean up, everyone moved into the library.

"What did Auntie have to say?" Elliot asked, wanting to know. He knew they had a whole lot of things to tell Baz and Rog before they headed back, but the fact that they had known who Emma was was driving him nuts.

"She gave us a quick rundown of what she's seen so far and what they've heard through their friends. There's corruption in the Convocation. Barry, specifically. We know two of his accomplices have been taken in, but she says he's still working behind the scenes. At least one is feeding him information and he's trying to get another Convocation member on his side. So far the new one he's interested in, isn't interested in his goals, but Auntie feels like Barry might force their hand somehow. She has a feeling that he might take someone close to them, something like that."

Gage took out his phone and sent Tom a quick text, letting him know to tell the Convocation members to lock down their loved ones. If it hadn't happened yet maybe they could stop it and cut off Barry's potential plan.

"She agrees he's holding people captive out west, she thinks southwest, but was having a hard time narrowing it down more than that. She said someone here is going to get taken or hurt, but wanted to reassure you that from what she's seen no one dies from our side. That's why she said you had to be changed by the time it got cold. Your ability to sense magic is going to be crucial and being more robust was needed. She didn't have anything specific though," Baz told them.

Gawain stood up, grabbing the pack of papers. "We made copies of some of the documents so your family would know what we've found. Maybe something in these will trigger a vision for her. This whole ordeal started with Barry's father.

He seemed to view collecting rare powers and paranormals as a goodwill type of thing. He was crazy, no doubt, but he firmly believed that he was keeping them safe and preserving them for the world. Part of that preservation would be continuing the line through procreation. He had forced breeding programs; if you didn't comply and have sex with who he assigned you to, your food was taken away.

"Barry isn't as noble intentioned in his kidnapping. We aren't completely sure what his goal is, but from the few notes and writings we've seen, it's not keeping them safe. We think that he is trying to get a true immortal to share their power with him. He still has a breeding program, but he uses cash as an incentive, so at least they're not being forced."

"Those aren't real though," Rog protested.

When Doc went to speak, Gage minutely shook his head. Elliot wasn't sure why and he would be asking his partner later. "They are," Gage told them. "The true immortals are one-of-a-kind paranormals, not like the Fae who can survive quite a bit but can still be killed with a lot of effort. There is only one of each at a time. If they form family bonds like a Clan or a Tribe with those they trust and perform a certain ritual, they could share that immortality with others. It's a very hard-to-find spell at this point." He had made sure of that.

"How do you know for sure?" Baz asked. Elliot could tell by the look on his cousin's face that he had a suspicion as to the answer.

"I am one," Gage said simply.

20

'*Why not let Doc speak?*' Elliot asked Gage as he brushed his teeth.

'*He's been hiding his whole life. He would speak for the benefit of the Clan, but this was one I could easily take. Plus, your family was bound to find out about me sooner or later. I don't want Doc feeling like he had to or doing something that made him uncomfortable,*' Gage replied, standing at the other sink also brushing his teeth.

The evening had been good. And hard. And loud. His cousins had been very loud right after Gage dropped his little bomb but had eventually settled down enough that they could finish talking and exchanging information. He and Gage had followed them back into town, eager to stay at Gage's house. He loved his Nightwood family, but he liked having their own place to go to each night. Gage's house felt like home.

Elliot still wasn't sure how he was supposed to help. He was also terrified of having one of his new family members hurt or kidnapped. At least they were all immortal thanks to Doc's ritual, but if Barry found that out, any one of them would be a goldmine to him. Of course, Doc himself would need to perform the ritual but Barry might not know that, or he could try to get the information of how to do it out of them. Elliot didn't really know the details, but he was sure some of them knew. Gage was the one who had found the spell and ended up passing it on to Doc. None of them would share how it worked, but if there had been one copy out there, who was to say there wasn't another. Or maybe someone else who knew how would share it to protect a loved one. Barry didn't seem like he had many scruples when it came to what he would or wouldn't do to get to his goal.

"Stop worrying. We can't do anything about it now. I sent a warning over the forum, but I can't do much else to make sure they stay safe other than help stop Barry," Gage told him, stepping up behind him and wrapping his arms around his waist.

Elliot looked at them in the mirror, loving how Gage's height and skin contrasted against his.

"I love you," he said, leaning his head back and turning slightly so he could kiss Gage, loving how those gray eyes softened at the words.

"I love you too," Gage said, bending slightly to grab Elliot in a bridal carry. Elliot laughed as his man threw him onto the bed and he bounced on the landing. Gage crawled up to him, straddling his hips, leaning down to press a kiss to his lips, his hardened cock pressing against Elliot.

Elliot gave his cousins another hug as they prepared to climb back into their car to leave.

"You got everything you need?" he asked. Baz nodded, holding his box of baked goods tightly. He had such a sweet tooth. "You'll have to come back after all this is done. The Christmas market is supposed to be amazing. Auntie would love the museum."

"Sounds good. I've missed you," Baz said, bumping their shoulders together.

"Be careful, cuz," Rog said, giving him a fist bump before climbing into the passenger seat.

Baz put the pastry box in the back seat and even buckled it in, giving it a fond pat before closing the door.

"Call if you need us. I'll pass everything on. It doesn't sound good, watch your back," he warned.

Elliot nodded. He swallowed a scream as Marco suddenly popped in next to him.

"We've got an issue. Can't put a finger on who or where they are, but someone is circling the town. They weren't here the other day, so I'm not sure if they're trying to follow your cousins out or not. But I think we need to err on the side of caution with the documents they're bringing back," Marco advised.

"What do you recommend?" Baz asked. "Our car is spelled to resist spells and tracking."

"Hm. If they can move fast enough, they could track you the old-fashioned way. Or if they managed to get ahead of you, they could still cause an issue with any bridges or the road itself, which would be a physical problem for you not a magical one per se. You'd still be stuck dealing with them. I can transport you home," Marco offered.

"I can't really leave the car here," Baz said, regretfully.

"Eh, it's not a problem. Climb in," Marco told him. "Give me a minute and I'll be right with you."

Marco walked over to Gage. "I have a couple of leads I'm going to check out once I get them home. Gawain found a couple properties that might match our criteria," he told his brother.

"Be careful. Let me know what you find," Gage said, grabbing Marco in a quick, hard hug.

"Will do." Marco gave them all a nod, climbed into the back seat of the car and placed his hands on both of Elliot's cousins' shoulders. They poofed out, with Rog's gasp the only sound in the air.

Elliot's phone dinged as he was walking back into the house.

BAZ: That was crazy. I wish I could get around that quickly all of the time. Be safe.

ELLIOT: You too.

"They made it home safely," Elliot told Gage as they sat down in the living room with everyone else.

"Gawain, do you know where Marco is going tonight?" Gage asked worriedly. He didn't like that someone was watching the town.

"If it's the three properties I gave him earlier, then yes. All of them are right around Nevada and Arizona. I'll have a few more in New Mexico and Texas soon. I'm tracking down a few more old deeds for those. I want to make sure they fit what we're looking for before I send anyone out. The last thing we need is drawing attention to our search by someone calling the cops on a trespasser."

Gage nodded. He was glad someone knew where Marco would be going. He was worried with Elliot's aunt's message that one of them would be taken. Marco would be on his guard of course and had thousands of years' worth of experience, but he was still Gage's little brother. He could still see the small squirmy baby that he had been.

"Thanksgiving is coming up. Does everyone have time to do a quick plan?" Emma asked.

Gage had actually taken the evening off so he could join in. They'd brought him a plate last year, but this year he had wanted to actually be there. One of his deputies had the evening shift as his family celebrated earlier in the day. Gage would be on call for emergencies, but those were few and far between now.

"I vote for lots of food," Ian said, grinning.

Emma laughed, shaking her head. "What kinds though?"

she asked. "Do we want to do it like last year, or do we want to try something different?"

"For us newbies, what was last year?" Elliot asked.

"So much food. We had the football game on, played some boardgames, watched a movie in the evening," Shaye told him.

"We had turkey and brisket for the proteins, rolls, mashed and sweet potatoes, green beans. Emma made pies for dessert," Sam added.

"Can you make your Brussels Sprouts?" Elliot asked Shaye. He didn't like most Brussels Sprouts, but he loved hers. "I'll make a pumpkin roll," he added as a bribe. He knew Shaye loved the pumpkin cake rolled with cream cheese frosting.

"Deal," she said with a grin.

"What about you Gage? Is there anything specific you want?" Emma asked him.

"It was all delicious last year, so I'm good with anything," he replied. He and Marco hadn't really celebrated Thanksgiving much. They got together and ate, but sometimes it was a couple of frozen pizzas. They didn't really do fancy or even sit-down dinners all that often. They hadn't been raised with that as the norm and neither of them were great cooks. He normally grabbed a pumpkin pie and a container of whipped cream for dessert, but that was usually the most Thanksgiving-y thing they had.

"Same time as last year? Three o'clock work for everyone? Do you think Marco can make it or should we adjust the time?"

"I'll let him know. If he comes later, we can save a plate for him. With this investigation going on, I wouldn't schedule something around him," Gage replied. It was sweet Emma wanted to make sure he was included, but Marco might be called out on a case and end up being late or leaving early.

"Do I have to eat sweet potatoes?" Jimmy asked Marge, a

bit of disgust in his voice. Gage thought he had been trying to whisper it, but they all had great hearing. He watched as Duncan bit his lip, trying not to laugh.

"No, you can eat what you want, as long as you get some protein and vegetables," Marge told him softly. "Not just pie."

"Pumpkin is like a vegetable," Jimmy protested.

"Not with all the sugar added to make it a dessert," Marge said firmly.

Gage snorted at that one. Jimmy had really gotten comfortable in his spot in the family and was just beginning to test boundaries. Nothing major, he was such a good kid, but a little pushback here and there. Which was to be expected, he was at the right age for that.

He settled back into the couch, Elliot leaning against his side as they watched Jimmy try to win his argument.

21

Gage awoke, smelling coffee and baking sugar. Hmmm. Reaching over, Elliot's side of the bed was cold, so he must have been up for a while. He couldn't believe he didn't wake up when Elliot left the bed, although they were up pretty late last night. He threw some clean clothes on after brushing his teeth and reapplying deodorant, figuring that since they had taken a bath right before bed, he could skip the shower this morning.

He stood in the doorway, watching his mate dance to the music he had playing on his phone. Elliot was dressed in loose gray sweatpants and a simple white t-shirt, but he looked delicious. Gage licked his lips, wondering if he could talk him back into bed. You would think after last night, he would be sated, but he craved Elliot. Nothing had been like this. He had had his hookups in the past, but no one had ever grabbed his attention, his heart, and his lust all at the same time. Elliot was his friend, family, and lover all in one.

"Come in and grab coffee, love. The cinnamon rolls are on the table, they should still be warm. There's more icing drizzle for them on the stove if you want more. I just need to roll the cake before it cools. And no nookie this morning! I have to get this done first," Elliot scolded.

Gage's hand stopped inches from Elliot's round cheeks. He hadn't even been looking at him, how had he known?

"I smelled you," Elliot said, laughing. "Eat and once I finish this cake, we can get on with your plan."

Gage kissed the back of Elliot's neck, loving the shiver that went through him. He sat though, being good. He grabbed a cinnamon roll, a moan escaping when the flavors hit his tongue. It was so good, warm and gooey, sweet but with the right amount of cinnamon to balance it. The icing had a slight tang as well, so he thought it was a cream cheese icing. Looking up, he noticed Elliot had stopped what he was doing, his spatula still dripping icing, to stare at him. Dropping the utensil, Elliot prowled toward him, throwing a leg across his lap to straddle his legs. Leaning down, he licked the icing off Gage's lips, groaning as he felt Gage's cock fill and press against his waist.

"How long do you need for the cake?" Gage asked, his voice rough.

Elliot slowly rotated his hips, gently pressing against his cock. "It has to cool, so I have a little bit of time." He bit back a scream as Gage suddenly stood, his hands cupped under Elliot's ass to hold him. As he stood all the way up, he pressed a kiss to Elliot's lips before sucking on the hot spot behind his ear. Slowly letting Elliot slide down his body until he was standing, Gage pressed his hips against Elliot, teasing them both.

"Go get on the bed. I'll be there in a minute," Gage ordered, his voice husky with desire.

As soon as Elliot was gone, Gage moved toward the stove, grabbing the left-over homemade drizzle for the rolls. Entering their room, his cock filled as he took in the sight of Elliot spread out on the bed, completely naked. His pale skin had a smattering of freckles, his muscles were lean but defined. Gage licked his lips as he watched his mate slowly stroking his own cock. It was a good size, average but thick, cut.

Gage walked over to the bed, slowly running one hand over the smooth skin. "Close your eyes for me," he instructed, wanting Elliot to focus on the sensations.

As those pretty blue eyes closed, Gage tested the temperature of the icing, making sure it was warm but wouldn't burn his lover. Tilting the pan slightly, he drizzled a zigzag down Elliot's stomach, loving how his breath caught and his stomach muscles clenched. So pretty. Bending down, his tongue traced the icing trail, leading right to Elliot's cock. Ignoring the whimper as he stopped licking, Gage tilted the pan again, decorating Elliot's inner thighs. The icing was sweet against the slight saltiness of his skin, the leg hairs rasping against Gage's tongue. Hmm, what to do next, he wondered.

He grinned a little evilly as he poured some of the warm icing into his hand and used it to coat his mate's balls. Elliot's gasp as his balls were dunked into the heat made him smile. He blew on the icing, loving the shiver that went through his mate. When there was almost a crust on top of the icing over his skin, Gage drizzled more icing around Elliot's cock, licking it slowly with his tongue, but never taking it fully into his mouth. When Elliot thrust trying to get deeper in Gage's mouth, he pulled back. Gage knelt on the floor in front of the bed, opening his mouth to blow a warm stream of air across the still iced balls in front of him.

"Please," Elliot pleaded, his hands clenching the sheet on either side of him.

Gage opened his mouth wide, taking the sweet treats into his mouth, his tongue washing the icing off his mate. When he was satisfied Elliot's sac was clean, he leaned back. "Flip over, hands and knees," he demanded, eager to pleasure his mate. "Keep your eyes closed."

As Elliot knelt on the edge of the bed, his shoulders down, firm ass in the air, Gage leaned forward and inhaled deeply. He loved the smell of his mate, that lemony scent got to him every time. Standing up and taking his place between Elliot's legs, he saw he was running low on the icing. Bending over, he pressed gentle kisses to Elliot's back, licking and kissing his way down. As he reached the slope of Elliot's little bubble butt, Gage reached for the icing again.

"Grab your cheeks please," he told his mate, nipping at one cheek.

Elliot reached back, a hand on either side pulling his cheeks apart, his head lying on the bed, eyes still closed. Gage groaned. Elliot didn't have much hair back here, and he could see the wrinkled skin clearly. Dipping the pan down, he let a small stream of icing flow down his lover's crack, darting forward to lick across his hole.

"Oh god! What are you...are you licking my ass? No, don't stop, do that again," Elliot demanded when Gage pulled away to get a breath.

Gage grinned, happy he could be the one to introduce rimming to his mate. He drizzled the remaining icing, lapping it up. As he twirled his tongue, he could feel Elliot's entrance softening, relaxing under the pleasure. Gage reached out with one hand, never removing his tongue, to grab the lube from the nightstand. As his tongue speared into Elliot's channel, his love let out a guttural moan.

"Please Gage... I need...more... In me... Fuck me please. Now!" Elliot panted, desperate to come.

Gage flipped open the lube with one hand and squirted out a large dollop. As he tried to smear it around his fingers, he vaguely thought they would need to change the sheets as half of it fell to the bed. He quickly slid two fingers in, stretching Elliot to take him. He was still tight even after being rimmed. Easing a third finger in, Gage scissored his fingers.

"Now! Get in me now!" Elliot demanded, thrusting back on his hand, gasping as fingers grazed his prostate.

Gage nipped his cheek before standing and applying more lube to his own dick. He normally liked to get four fingers in Elliot before fucking him, but they were both desperate to come now. He still took his time, pausing once the head was inside giving Elliot time to adjust.

"Gage, if you don't fuck me now, I'm going to lose my freaking mind," Elliot said, turning his head to look at him, his eyes wild and desperate.

Slamming his hips forward, Gage bottomed out, his balls gently resting against Elliot's. Grabbing his lover's hips, holding him tightly, Gage drew his hips back, hammering his body back into Elliot's, both of them moaning at the sensation. He knew he wouldn't last long, his mate felt too good around him; warm, tight, the sounds Elliot was making were driving him nuts. Gage wanted his lover to come first and he made sure his dick hit deep and hard with each stroke.

"Oh god, oh god," Elliot chanted, his hands grasping at the sheets. "Please, please, please…"

Gage adjusted his stance just a smidge so he nailed Elliot's prostate on the next stroke. He bared his teeth in a feral grin as his man screamed out his orgasm, coming hands-free, his cum coating the bed underneath him. Gage roared out his own release seconds later, the tightness of Elliot's body pulling him over. The air was filled with the scent of their sweat and their heavy breathing.

"I'm going to get the bath started," he said, kissing Elliot's shoulder. He gently pulled out, easing Elliot to lie on his side away from the puddle. He'd change the sheets while Elliot soaked.

He hummed a little song as he filled the tub with hot water and a bath oil. Happy Thanksgiving to him.

Elliot carried the two pumpkin rolls up the driveway as Gage carried some sodas and wine. They had made sure to get some root beer for Jimmy. He normally didn't get to drink soda and they thought it would be a nice treat for him. Gage was trying hard to be the cool uncle; he didn't see his brother having kids anytime soon, so Jimmy would be the only child to spoil for a while. Unless the Nightwood Clan family decided to have some children, although they would probably wait until this issue with Barry was finished. Plus, paranormals had a hard time getting pregnant for the most part. Elliot had found this really fun-looking puzzle book that they were bringing along too. Jimmy was so easy to make happy. He was a great kid.

"Hey, Uncle Gage and Uncle Elliot! You should see the turkey! It's huge. Like it takes up a whole oven by itself," Jimmy exclaimed as he threw open the door as they walked up the stairs. "Are those cake? They look like round cake," he said, looking closely at the pumpkin rolls.

Elliot laughed. Someone may have gotten into something with sugar already or he was really excited for Thanksgiving.

"It is cake. You roll it right after it comes out of the oven and then when it cools, you unroll and spread on the icing and roll back up. Pretty cool, huh?"

"Does it taste good?" Jimmy asked.

"I think so," Elliot replied.

"I had the trimmings. It's really good," Gage confided in a conspiratorial tone.

"Hey guys, dinner's almost ready," Ian said, coming into the room. "Did ye need help? There are coolers for drinks on the back porch."

Gage handed him the soda boxes, following him out to the porch to put the red wine in a cooler with the beers for now. He knew the girls liked their wine cold.

"Is Marco here yet?" he asked, not having seen his brother on his way through the house.

"No' yet," Ian replied. "He did send a message to Rolf earlier, saying he might be late."

Nodding, Gage followed Ian back into the house. He hoped his brother would be able to come, everything smelled delicious.

"Where is everyone?" he asked, noticing how empty the house seemed. He could hear them somewhere, but only Shaye, Emma, and Doc were in the kitchen checking on a few things.

"Watching the football game," Shaye said, looking up from the massive turkey she was basting. When she saw him looking toward the living room, she added, "They moved to the theater room. Sam was able to hook the TV in and there's more seating. Elliot just headed down there, if you want to join them."

"Come on, it's just down the hallway," Ian told him, leading the way. They passed Tess in the hall.

"Hey, Gage! I hope you came hungry. We may have overdone it. There are snacks in there too. I need to grab the rolls out of the oven, and I'll be right back," she said.

As he entered the room, he realized that he hadn't been in here yet. He'd been pretty much everywhere else, but they used the living room for a lot of the get-togethers. This room was nice, the windows covered by thick curtains to blackout the room if needed, a large screen to project movies on, comfortable leather theater chairs, set out in two rows in front of the screen. There was an old-school popcorn machine in the back, probably where the smell of fresh popcorn was coming from. There was a small candy and chip display as well. A Keurig coffee machine with a tower of pods stood atop of a mini fridge.

He grabbed a drink and sat next to Elliot. He wondered why they didn't use this room more often.

'Rolf said the curtains just got installed last week. There had been a mix-up in the orders and it took a while to sort out. Plus, he

added more chairs so there would be enough seats for all of us,' Elliot told him. *'I think game night will still be in the living room though.'*

Doc called out from the kitchen a few minutes later, letting them know the rest of the food was ready. Gage handed Elliot a plate and got in line, his stomach growling at the smells. He had just taken a bite of mashed potatoes when his brother popped in.

"Sorry, I'm late. I was finishing up a few things for tomorrow," Marco apologized.

"Are you following up on those sites I sent you?" Gawain asked.

"Yeah. I have a few the Convocation wants me to check out too. I'll probably be gone a week, but I should still make it back for the next Inebriated Inconsistencies night. I'm going to do my best to make it, I don't want to miss it," Marco said, grinning.

"Do you want me to research the sites they gave you?" Gawain asked.

Marco shook his head. "I did a quick search on them, and they seem to fit the criteria. They're all in the states we were looking at, so I might as well fly over them on my way to your places. I'll have my phone with me if something looks fishy and I can always reach Gage through our link."

22

G age knew he was scowling at his phone, but he couldn't make himself stop. Marco was due hours ago, but he wasn't here, and he wasn't responding to his phone calls. It was frankly starting to worry him. Tonight was the first time that Marco would be attending an Inebriated Inconsistencies night with the Clan, and he had been super excited to come. He had made sure it was in his calendar so he wouldn't forget.

Gage tried reaching out over their telepathic link but was met with a blank space. He'd never run into anything like it before and it was freaking him out.

Elliot leaned into him. "Still can't reach him?" he asked quietly.

Gage shook his head.

"You should see if Rolf can help, somehow. He has telepathy as his gift, so maybe he can help boost you or something," he suggested.

"It wouldn't hurt to ask." Gage shrugged, getting up to find Rolf. He had been in the kitchen last time he saw him.

Turning the corner, Gage almost ran into him. "Hey, sorry about that. I was looking for you. I can't get ahold of Marco and at this point his phone goes straight to voicemail. Which has happened before, especially if he's working a case and doesn't want it to be heard. He normally finds time to check in though. The weirdest part, the part that is worrying me, is that I can't reach him over our link. I've never run into this before and wanted to see if you could try to boost me or see what you thought."

"Yeah, of course. I've linked with him before, so that should help. I'll link with you first, then you link with him, and we'll see what we get."

Gage felt and heard Rolf along the telepathic link and then he reached out to find his brother. Once again, he ran into blankness. There was no connection on the other side, or rather it was like it was blocked. He felt Rolf sending his own power through him, bolstering his signal as it were, but nothing changed. Rolf changed his tactic, feeling his way around the link, searching for something.

"I've got nothing," Rolf finally admitted. "I haven't run into this before. I can tell you he's alive; it feels vastly different than when I tried to connect to a deceased person. I'm…" Rolf trailed off, clearly thinking something.

"What?" Gage demanded.

"I'm not positive, this is just a thought that entered my head and I have no real basis for it, so take it with a grain of salt. Do you remember when Marge was taken? We couldn't scent her or track her because she had a Tamer spell on her. What if he has something similar? I didn't try to connect telepathically with Marge at the time, so I can't be sure if I'm right."

Gage listened, horror spreading through him at the thought. "I have a pair of Tamer spelled cuffs at the office for extreme cases. I hate using them because it cuts a shifter off from their animal, which is horrible. Let me go get them, I'll put them on, and you can see if it feels the same."

Minutes later, he had the cuffs in hand and headed back to

the house. He gave his mate a quick warning that they would lose connection for a minute and handed Rolf the key. Slapping the cuffs on himself, Gage braced as his connection to his griffin waned. He could still feel him, but it was much fainter than normal.

Rolf stared at him, head tilted. "It's crazy. You're standing right there, so close I can actually touch you, but you're not registering to my other senses. It's like a blank wall trying to reach you as well. If Marco isn't in something with a Tamer spell, he's in something very similar because it feels alike," he said, sympathy in his face.

"Crap."

"Do you have any idea of how we can find him? Did they train you with anything like this at the Convocation?" Rolf asked, working on getting the cuffs off.

Gage shook his head. They had gone over how and why to use cuffs spelled with a Tamer spell, but that was it. He guessed they never thought about what would happen if the spell were put on a Warden in the line of duty.

Elliot walked over, wrapping an arm around Gage's waist. "Can you try tracing him with your magic?" he asked. "Don't you have a tracking magic?"

"I do, but the Tamer spell would block that. I tried with Marge without success and I'm not registering a trail to Marco at all," Gage replied.

"Head to the library. I'm gathering everyone up. We're going to figure out a game plan on how to get Marco back. My guess is Barry somehow got him and he's probably at the stupid compound we can't find," Rolf told him, urging them to the library.

'Family meeting, library. Marco's missing.' Elliot heard Rolf say over the Nightwood Clan link. He startled, having never really heard the link used other than the first time it was created.

It took a few minutes, as Sam, Ian, and Berkley were in town.

"What's going on?" Berkley asked as they ran into the room.

"Let me wait until everyone's here," Rolf said. Once everyone entered the room and sat down, he spoke up.

"Marco is missing. It's probably safe to assume it has to do with the property searches he was conducting and with Barry in particular. Gage can't contact him or trace him, and his phone is off. We think Marco has a Tamer spell on him," Rolf explained. "We need to come up with a game plan and find him."

Gawain pulled out a map, laying it on the table. He grabbed bright pink Post-It tabs, placing down five of them. They were scattered around the southwest, which was no surprise. "These are the locations I gave Marco. Now, he had others from the Convocation, but I don't know where those are. Gage, can you reach out to your contact and see what he knows? I'll call Rob and have him check in with his as well."

Gage nodded, pulling out his phone and walking over to a corner.

"Tom? Gage. I need your help. Marco was investigating some properties last week and seems to have gone missing. I can't reach him at all. He had been searching some properties, including ones on the request of the Convocation. Can you send me where those were?"

"I have no idea what you're talking about," Tom said. "What properties?"

"He had a list of properties that fit the criteria we've been searching for from Gawain. When he was here at Thanksgiving, he mentioned he was also going to search a few that the Convocation had asked him to look into."

"Fuck," Tom cursed. "Did he mention who gave him the information?"

"No. You really don't know anything about this?" Gage

asked, frustrated, running a hand over his head and clenching his fist so he wouldn't yell.

"No, I do not. I'm going to get into the office and see what I can find. I'll let you know as soon as I hear anything. If you need help, you call in any Wardens you know you can trust. We take care of our own. I gotta go," Tom said, hanging up.

Gage shut his eyes, taking deep breaths to calm down. He can't die, he reminded himself. Of course, that didn't stop injury or torture, his brain reminded him. He felt a hand on his arm, his body calming. Opening his eyes, he saw Shaye looking at him in concern.

"We'll find him. I may not be able to track him, but I can heal him when we find him," she promised. "You guys are family. We're going to get him back."

She drew him back to the group where Elliot took his hand, sending him feelings of love over their bond.

"Tom didn't know anything about the other locations. He says the Convocation didn't request any searches. He's going into the office to see what he can find," Gage told them.

"Rob's reaching out to his contact using an emergency code, so we should hear back soon," Gawain added.

"What else do we know?" Berkley asked.

"Not much, other than the sites were in the same states we were already looking in," Gawain replied.

Well, that wasn't going to help much.

23

Dropping his head to smack against his desk, Gage tried not to feel a sense of hopelessness. It had been two weeks since they had realized Marco was missing. He still couldn't sense his brother.

Tom hadn't found any trace of an official Convocation request being sent out and no one in his group of trusted people knew anything about it. Rob's contact also confirmed it wasn't official but was doing some digging into files in an attempt to find a trail, which Gage read as hacking into other people's computers. They had started with Brandon, which would be an obvious suspect other than the fact that Marco probably wouldn't have trusted him. Gage was very much afraid that there was another Barry mole in the organization somewhere.

He had reached out to his contacts and fellow Wardens that he trusted. No one had heard of anything or been asked to check out other sites from someone in the Convocation. No one had seen Marco either. They seemed to have been the last ones to see him at Thanksgiving. It was an odd feeling not being able to sense his brother; his griffin had been pacing in his mind nonstop since they realized what was wrong. He was ashamed to say he didn't catch it immediately. The link had always been in the back of his mind, but he hadn't noticed right away when it went silent. Now that he knew it was gone after more than a thousand years, he wasn't reacting well to the loss. He knew logically that his brother was still alive, Rolf kept checking for him, but his griffin was mourning like he was gone. He might have to ask Rolf to connect with his griffin to reassure the animal because he was pretty much useless like this.

Looking down, he tried to focus on the paperwork he was supposed to finish today. He needed to finalize a time-off request from Doug. He wanted to give Doug the time off but was hoping that it didn't overlap with anything from this case. He would be there personally to help search any sites that came up. Maybe he could get a fellow Warden to hang out nearby in case he needed to leave so his deputies weren't stretched too thin. He and Jack went back pretty far and had helped each other out in the past. He knew most, if not all, of the Nightwood Clan would be coming and he didn't want to leave the town unprotected, even with the wards. If they were all gone, it was the perfect time for Barry to try to get through the protections. There were other paranormals in town, which Barry didn't know about. Maybe he could give them a heads-up when they would be gone. The Yougers were witches, and even though their magic was mostly plant and animal based, they could still help.

The only plus in this whole thing had been in the forum. Eventually everyone had checked in and verified they were safe. They all swore to take more precautions and Gage had shared a basic protection spell that he thought most, if not all, of them would be able to use.

"I have an idea!" Berkley shouted as he ran in. "Gage, get the Tamer handcuffs and meet us in the backyard at home. I'm going to get some things ready." He ran back out of the Sheriff's station as quickly as he arrived.

Okay then. Gage hurriedly finished the paperwork, not wanting to let his employees down. He reached into his bottom drawer, his magic unlocking the door. He grabbed the cuffs, tucking them into his back pocket.

"Doris, I'm heading over to Rolf's, if you need me. Sean is out patrolling, and Doug will be in this evening," Gage said as he headed out.

"Still no word on your brother?" she asked. "You'll find him. We can hold down the fort here if you need us to," she said when he shook his head.

"Thanks. I don't know what I would do without you guys," he said with a small smile. He really did have the best crew.

As he left the building, he saw Ian locking up the Winged Potter.

"Need a lift?" he asked, pulling the car over.

"Sure, thanks," Ian said as he climbed in. "Doc had a few more patients, but Tess headed over. Shaye's helping Doc finish up, but Berkley said he needed Tess for some magic maybe. Do ye ken whit's going on?" His mate was in such a hurry that he didn't say, and the only thing Ian could sense over their bond was a sense of anticipation and hope.

"No. He ran in, told me to grab the Tamer cuffs and come over. Then he ran out again," Gage replied, turning into the driveway and opening the gates.

"Huh. The only thing I can tell is that he's hopeful about something," Ian said.

As they parked, Elliot joined them from the front of the house. "Do you know what's going on?" he asked.

Gage and Ian both shook their heads as they headed toward the backyard.

Tess, Rolf, Gawain, Merri, Marge, and Duncan were already there waiting with Berkley. Berkley was almost bouncing in excitement.

"Elliot, you can sense magic, correct?" Berkley asked.

When Elliot nodded, he asked a follow-up question. "Even the wards here?" As Elliot nodded again, Berkley grinned, a huge smile taking over his face.

"Here's what I'm thinking. We have one of us wear the Tamer spelled handcuffs and hide on the property. Your job will be to find them. If you can sense the Tamer spell, I'll put an additional concealment spell over them. If we can try to recreate the circumstances Marco might be being held in and get you trained to look for something similar, you might be able to find him. Our magic isn't working, but you see all magic, even ones meant to stay hidden."

"If I know what to look for, I can travel with you to search for Marco and I could tell you if there was a concealment or Tamer spell nearby. Which we could then follow up and search there for the hidden compound," Elliot said, excitement growing.

It would work, he knew in his soul it would work. This was why he was supposed to be here. His family finding him, becoming friends with Shaye, his aunt's visions. It was all leading to this. He may have doubted that Fate had a strong hand in his life before, but he could suddenly see all the pieces coming together. To stop Barry, the Nightwood Clan had to be formed first, all of these amazing people coming together with their unique gifts and talents, becoming a family. All of their connections would help bring everyone together and fill in the missing puzzle pieces.

"Yup," Berkley replied, grinning back at him. He was relieved to finally have a plan that could get Marco back. He only hoped it worked; he didn't have any other ideas of how to save him. "Who wants to hide first?"

Elliot collapsed on the couch, exhausted. They had worked for hours, long past when the sun went down. At first his senses tingled when a containment spell had been cast if he was close by, but as they moved him farther and farther away, he was able to fine tune his ability at detecting things. At one point, he had ended up on the edges of town to test the range of his power. It had made everyone on edge, but he even stood outside the town wards to work on sensing the differences between the town wards, the Clan house wards, and the separate containment spell around the person hiding wearing the Tamer spell. He made sure to have his Nightwood Clan pendant on just in case someone was watching the town's borders.

It took him a minute or twenty, but he was finally able to really distinguish between the magics. He had never really attempted to differentiate before, he just knew when magic was in play and there were wards. Now though, now he could at least tell when there were different kinds, and he was a pro at detecting the Tamer spell and pretty decent at sensing a containment spell. When he really paid attention, he realized that while all magic made him tingle, they each felt slightly different.

Right now though, he just wanted to eat and let his poor brain rest.

"Come on, babe. Emma has stew and sourdough ready," Gage told him, startling him awake. Elliot hadn't even realized his eyes had closed. "We'll eat and crash here tonight."

Elliot nodded, glad they had decided to keep a change of clothes here for emergencies. Hopefully he could stay awake long enough to eat.

24

Elliot sent a text to his mother. It was in code of course, just in case someone was monitoring outgoing messages from town. They were taking a road trip to look at a few locations that Rob's contact had uncovered during his search. The emails had been buried and deleted, but whoever Rob knew had been able to access the Convocation's servers and restore at least part of the messages. They were still trying to figure out who had sent Marco into a trap. That part had been pretty well destroyed, but it turned out that Daryl was a bit of a tech wizard, and he was going to take a look at them and see if he couldn't restore more of the emails or trace them back to where they originated. It did seem that it wasn't Brandon, which meant they had another traitor in the Convocation.

Baz was due in tonight and was driving the cloaked car. They were going to search a property in Texas first, as it was the closest. Their friends in Montana had arranged for a private plane; one of their family members had their own aircraft and would help them get around. It wasn't unusual for him to take random flights, so it shouldn't throw up any red flags. They had also arranged to have rental cars at the different airports, some of which they weren't even going to, just in case. It would still be quite the hike to drive to the places from an airport, but not all of them had a flying shifter side. And none of them had Marco's teleportation abilities.

If Texas was a dud, they would head west, stopping in New Mexico, Arizona, and Nevada. There were places to investigate at each one. There were a few in California that matched the description as well, but none of them thought Barry would be there.

Gage had brought in a friend, another Warden to watch over the town. Emma and Doc were staying back, as no one wanted Doc on Barry's radar. Marge was staying home as well with Jimmy. They had already called a town meeting and had informed everyone of when and why they were leaving. After the meeting, many of the paranormals in town came to speak to them and volunteered to help keep an eye on things.

Getting to the first airport would be a little tricky. They were going in waves just in case someone was watching. Baz was driving Rolf and Shaye in his car, Gawain and Duncan were flying. Sam, Tess, and Merri were taking the SUV. The one thing Elliot was excited about with this whole trip was that he would be flying with his mate for the first time. Gage was worried he wouldn't like it, or something, because he had repeatedly told him that if it was too much to tell him and he would land so Elliot could ride in the SUV.

As they got dressed this morning, Gage had made sure he had his pendant so he could fly without being seen. They were bringing Marco's pendant as well; Berkley had been blaming himself that Marco had been taken because he had forgotten to give it to him at Thanksgiving. Gage had told him it wasn't his fault; he had forgotten as well and without being used to wearing it, he had even forgotten to wear it himself most of the time. Elliot had caught Gage checking for Marco's pendant multiple times today. He thought his mate was more worried than he was letting on. They had no idea what condition they would find Marco in and if they had to sneak him out, the pendant would help protect him from any magical attacks. They still had not been able to confirm if Barry or his people had any special abilities that they needed to be worried about.

Elliot was closing the bakery while they were gone. Emma couldn't handle it all on her own and there wouldn't be anyone else to help. He would have a sale when he was back to make it up to everyone in town. Elliot sighed as he packed the last of his things in a bag. He had packed both him and Gage a duffle bag with toiletries, phone chargers, and clothes. It would be riding in the SUV. They had friends' houses along the way that they could stop and rest when needed. There were always hotels, but they were worried about the safety of those at the moment.

"Are you ready to go?" Gage asked. "Baz just pulled in."

"I am," he replied, moving to stand in front of his partner. He really just wanted a hug. He wasn't cut out for all this cloak and dagger stuff, but there was no way he wouldn't help find and rescue his mate's brother.

Gage must have seen something in his face or felt it through their bond because he pulled him in for a long tight hug. Elliot tucked his head into Gage's shoulder, loving how their heights were perfect for this. "We'll be fine. We have all sorts of magic users, Berkley's pendants, and Shaye's healing. Plus, we're all immortal at this point. If you need to get down or ride in the car—"

"I know. I'll let you know, I promise," Elliot told him. He took a deep breath in, letting the scent of his mate calm him down.

Gage hated bringing his mate into a dangerous situation, but Elliot's ability to sense magic would help them find Marco.

Even if Barry had built the compound to blend in with the landscape, Gage would imagine he'd also use a concealment spell. With the training they had done, Elliot would be able to tell them if he felt a Tamer or concealment spell. If nothing else, the guards should at least give off a magical signature.

His wings beat through the air carrying them toward the private airstrip. He held tight to Elliot, who was also attached by a harness. Gage hadn't wanted to take any chances of having to use his arms to fight anyone off or of Elliot falling asleep and letting go. Sam had laughed a bit and said it looked like a baby carrier, but it got the job done and Gage could relax a little bit.

He was watching the surrounding areas as they flew. He could see the taillights of the SUV and was making sure no one had tried to follow them. He had his friend Jack bring a scanner to make sure the cars hadn't had a tracking device on them, so if someone was following them it would be by sight only. The scanner found nothing, and it didn't look like they were being followed, which was good as they were coming up to the airstrip. He banked hard to the right, knowing he could shortcut and not follow the roads. Even with Elliot bundled up with hand warmers in his pockets and boots, he still worried about him being chilled. The air was cooler up here and it was December.

He hovered over the pavement, working his way slowly down, careful not to let it jar Elliot too much.

'I can't wait to stretch my legs, but that was amazing,' Elliot said. *'I want to do that again when we don't have a time limit. Maybe go fly over the park and see what we can see?'*

'That will be fun,' Gage replied. He had never really explored the park with someone else; he thought it would be fun to show Elliot all the little hidden waterfalls and his favorite spots. As soon as Elliot put his feet down and was steady, he reached around Gage's neck to release the harness. Gage switched back to his human form, pulling his mate in

for a hug. He wanted to make sure Elliot was warm enough. He saw Duncan and Gawain standing by a hangar, ready to go.

Headlights soon lit up the area as the cars pulled in. They were spaced apart by fifteen minutes or so, but it gave them time to walk around. The flyers were content to stand for a bit, but everyone else had ridden in the cars and were eager to stretch their legs. A bearded gentleman approached them, his eyes darting all around.

"Y'all the Nightwood Clan?" he asked.

Rolf stepped forward. "May I ask who's asking?" The lighting in the lot was dim and while they were in the meeting spot, Gage could tell Rolf wanted to be careful. Gage gave the stranger a quick scan, noting he was a shifter. He saw Berkley doing the same thing and gave a small nod to Rolf.

"Hector," the man replied, briefly using his phone to illuminate his face.

It matched the picture Daryl had sent them.

"Rolf. Nice to meet you," Rolf said, holding out a hand to shake. No one's pendants lit up and Gage could feel the sense of relief from everyone, even without the Clan bond.

"No one followed you here?" Hector asked them.

Gage shook his head. "I was watching from the air. There was no one else nearby."

"Alright, then let's get you guys going. I'm real sorry to hear about your brother being taken," Hector said. "This Barry guy has been a pain in the ass for years, but luckily my family hasn't been on his radar.

"I'm going to get you to Texas. There will be several rental cars available, pick which ones you want. Some of my cousins will be there to drive the other ones in different directions. There hasn't been any interest shown in the flights scheduled for the next several days, but we figured we'd err on the side of caution. My plane will take off after officially dropping off a mail package. Thorn will be your next pilot; he'll get you to New Mexico and Arizona. I have a couple of planes that I use for charters and mail runs. He's another cousin that works with me.

"I'll meet back up with you in Arizona. I have a regular client that needs dropping off there; it just so happens he's a federal agent and part of Rick's family. He's going to go with you on the Arizona and Nevada runs. He's heard a few stories out there and he volunteered to be backup for you guys. Rick's sending over his information," Hector told them.

"Thanks," Rolf said. Ian, Berkley, Sam, and Gawain had already grabbed the bags out of the car. Elliot was standing off to the side talking to Baz. Gage could feel the anticipation in his beast. He was ready to find his brother and bring him back home. After this, he really needed to encourage Marco to speed up the house search near Rockfort. He wanted his brother close.

It was a tight squeeze, but they managed to all fit in the plane. It was a decent-sized plane; most of the guys were just a little larger than average. Elliot grabbed his hand, even as he was still talking with Baz. When this was over, they should have Elliot's family down for a visit. Maybe after Christmas.

25

Gage held in the growl his beast wanted to release. It wasn't anyone's fault who was here. Two spots in Texas, three in New Mexico, four in Arizona, and even one right across the border in California. Nothing. They had come up with nothing. Other than a pot farm and an illegal meth lab, which Rick's uncle Leo had taken care of.

They had quite a few to look at in Nevada, but something was drawing his attention to the southwest of the state. His gut was telling him to look along the Utah/Arizona state line, to follow it straight west into Nevada. Hector had met them with a slightly bigger plane and with the addition of Leo, the extra seating was much appreciated.

"I know this is off plan, but can we fly over this area first? My gut is telling me something is there," Gage said, showing him the area on a map.

Hector looked at him, then shrugged. "Sure. I know a couple of people in the area where we could land and borrow a car if needed. I always trust my gut, so let's get a move on. I'll let everyone else know to be on standby."

Gage knew that some of the others were waiting closer to Las Vegas for news. Thorn had switched to a helicopter so he could land where they would need him. A few of Rick's and Daryl's family members had volunteered to help. Gage didn't want to put them in danger though, so they were only there as backup if they needed more people. He thought they might be about thirty or so minutes away by helicopter.

They crossed the border into Nevada. Berkley, Tess, Merri, and Elliot were searching out the windows as they got closer to where Gage wanted to look.

"Stop!" Elliot shouted.

"Can't really do that," Hector shouted back, amusement in his voice.

Elliot's face turned bright red. "Yeah. Knee-jerk reaction. There's something down there, right where we just flew over. There's definitely magic there, at least one containment spell and I'm pretty sure I can sense multiple Tamers as well."

Hector nodded, jotting down the coordinates. "Let me get us to a friendly spot to land and I'll send the coordinates to the others. I know we can borrow a van that will get us there."

Gage looked down, trying to connect to his brother again, sending positive thoughts. Nothing that would give their intentions or location away, just in case someone could monitor it. His heart sped up; this was it, he knew it was. He could only hope that Marco was okay.

Rolf looked over at him sharply. "We'll get him and bring him home. He's still alive." Gage had forgotten that Rolf could tell the difference between trying to connect with someone who was blocked and someone who had died. Right now he needed that reassurance. It didn't matter that he knew that Marco was immortal, the base part of his brain feared the worst.

After Hector landed the plane and collected a van from a waiting friend, they drove to the meeting spot they had set up with the rest of their party. It was on some abandoned land close enough for them to reach the compound relatively quickly, but not so close that Barry or his guards would notice. They drove in without headlights, wanting to keep any signs of themselves to a minimum. Luckily, they all had great eyesight. As they waited for their backups, including Rick who was a Sheriff in Montana, Gage had to rein in his beast. He wanted to leave everyone else behind and tear through the earth to find his brother, his packmate. The human part of Gage knew that was a horrible idea and gritted his teeth in an effort to keep his beast contained.

'Hey. It's only a few more minutes,' Elliot tried to soothe him, rubbing a hand across his back. *'I know you want to get there as quickly as you can, but it will be better for everyone there if we have more than one person charging in. He might have guards who could start moving or killing people while you were distracted,'* he pointed out.

Gage nodded, knowing he was right but still wishing the others would hurry up. A few minutes later, he heard the rhythmic thump-thump-thump of helicopter blades coming closer. He was surprised to see both Rick and Daryl jump down from the helicopter, along with a few paranormals he didn't recognize. He took a deep breath, letting a trickle of his magic flow out, trying to sense what they were.

Holy shit. His gaze flew to the man who had just climbed out. He was huge, even larger than Gage himself, and lord knows he wasn't small. This man had to be seven-foot tall, and he was solid muscle.

'Phoenix,' his beast whispered in awe.

Gage shut his mouth and headed over to introduce himself, eager to meet another rare paranormal.

"Thanks for coming. I'm Gage," he said, shaking every-one's hands. As he got to the man, he felt a small tendril of questioning magic lick at his skin.

Smiling, he nodded at the other shifter. He could feel their beasts looking at each other. It was always a dance of some kind when he met other rare paranormals. No one really knew who they could trust and they were always on edge. He hoped he could put this man's mind at ease. Pulling out one of his magicked cards, he breathed over the top, activating the spell. He passed it over to the phoenix shifter.

"There's a safe place for us, if you would like to talk to others," he said. "As soon as I let go, the card will destroy itself." It was his way of being able to pass the information along without speaking about it directly in case someone was listening and also not letting the knowledge of the forum fall into the wrong hands.

The man looked startled, staring at the card in surprise. "I've heard of this," he admitted. "I have a friend… This is yours?"

Gage nodded. "It's hard to find information and I wanted to share what I had. When I come across someone who can benefit, I try to let them know." He didn't want to give too much information away since he wasn't sure if the man had come out as a rare to the other people here.

"I'm Neil," the phoenix told him.

"The Nightwood Clan are my family, my adopted Flight," Gage told him, trying to let him know that they could be trusted. Letting go of the card, he motioned Elliot to come over. "And this is my mate, Elliot."

"Nice to meet you," Elliot said, nodding at the shifter.

"I heard about your problems and wanted to help. I'm a doctor and have some healing abilities. Rick is my nephew and had nothing but good things to say about you," Neil said.

"Thank you. He's been a good friend. They did tell you what the problem is, right?" Gage wanted to make sure the man knew of the danger before he got too close to the compound.

"They did but thank you for asking."

"Berkley! Can you come here a minute?" Gage yelled.

"Hey, what do you need?" Berkley asked as he came over.

Gage knew Berkley could sense the magic in the other man and was curious.

"Neil could use some help staying off Barry's radar when we go in," Gage said simply.

"Oh! Of course. Do you have a necklace, a bracelet, or something?" Berkley asked Neil.

"I have a watch," Neil said slowly, looking confused, holding out a wrist.

Berkley studied it quickly. "That's perfect. May I borrow it for a minute?"

Neil handed it over, watching curiously as Berkley cast a concealment spell and a bit of light flared.

"This will register you as human to other paranormals. I don't want to use too much energy to fine tune it right now, but I can always do that after. For now, Barry won't know you're a paranormal," Berkley said, handing it back.

"Thanks?" Neil replied, a slight question in his voice. Berkley smiled, gave them a nod, and then went back over to where Rick was talking to Rolf and Shaye.

Neil put the watch back on and Gage swallowed a laugh as half the group suddenly turned their heads toward them.

"What was that?" Neil asked Gage, as his family all stormed over to check on him.

"We've had some experience with Barry and his hunters," Gage explained. He pulled out his pendant. "Berkley has made ones for all of us. Because Barry already knew us, ours hides us from human hunters, but we register as paranormals to other paranormals. Mine, as well as someone else we know, hides our shifter side. Barry is a threat to all paranormals, but especially ones with rare gifts or who shift into one-of-a-kind beings.

"The last thing we need to do is have you on Barry's radar in case this doesn't go the way we want it to," Gage added.

"Maybe you should stay back," a worried voice said, coming up to stand next to Neil.

"I'll be fine," Neil protested. "Especially with my new watch. I'm meant to be here, Rick," he said firmly.

"Okay, gather up," Leo instructed. "I looked into old databases and found what I could about this place, which is not a lot. A land deed, but no mention or filings for building permits or anything like that. Which would make sense if they're staying off the grid. We're going to get close and wait. I'll shift and head in to see what I can."

"Won't you be noticed?" Sam asked.

Leo grinned as he shook his head. "I'm a snake; my natural counterparts are close to here, so I'll be able to blend in. I do have a concealment spell, so I register as a regular snake. It helps in my job.

"Anyway, I'll scope it out and report back. I'd like to get all the exits and entrances that we can see covered. From what you all shared, it doesn't seem like there will be a lot of them, probably to limit escape chances for the people he kidnapped, but it will also limit escape routes for Barry. If one of our flying shifters could take position above the compound to look for any other escape attempts we may miss, I'd appreciate it.

"Daryl has earpieces for everyone to wear so we can communicate. Even if you're in shifted form, at least you'll be able to hear what is going on," Leo added as Daryl stepped forward.

"I'll be in the air," Gawain volunteered. "I can tell Merri what's happening, and she can pass it on." They hadn't told the others about their blood bond Clan/Tribe links, so it would seem odd for him to be able to tell anyone else. After everyone got fitted with the earpieces, Leo went behind the van to undress so he could shift. Moments later they saw a rattlesnake move their way.

Gage could just barely make out the tiny earpiece magically attached to the Mojave rattlesnake's head.

"It's a bit of a trek for a snake to get to the compound

quickly. How about I fly you over and I can keep an eye out from the air while you look around. I can give word to Merri when the rest should make their way in and communicate a plan," Gawain offered.

Leo's snake gave a nod and Gawain gave Merri a quick kiss before changing. The snake carefully wrapped itself around the hawk's leg, the talons gently holding the curled-up tail end of the snake. It was an odd sight for sure, but it should get Leo close to the compound without setting off any warnings.

As they flew off, the rest of them finished introducing themselves. There was talk about fighting in human or shifted form for the shifters. It seemed to be a mix. Gage was planning to stay in his human form. He knew Sam would shift to his wolf; he had been training with Ian in human form, but still felt more comfortable fighting as a wolf. He thought Duncan might be a mix of both. The dragon fire could come in useful, but not many spaces were large enough for him to maneuver through if fully shifted.

"They just got there," Merri said a minute later. "Leo is working his way around the sides, Gawain is in the air. It doesn't seem like there's anyone outside that he can see. There's an old walled-in outdoor area, but it looks over-grown. He doesn't think it's been used in quite a while, but it matches the letter's description. There's a vehicle under a camouflage tarp, so Barry is probably there."

It was a few more minutes before Merri spoke again. "Leo showed Gawain a hidden exit in the back, so it looks like there is only the front door and a hidden rear door. The over-grown outdoor area could be an escape option if someone could get over the wall. They want us to come over, some through the back door, some through the front. Gawain will keep an eye from the air."

They loaded into the van, Hector staying with the heli-copter. He would fly it over when needed. Daryl was coming with them in the van, but he would be staying with it once they parked. He was going to be using it as a command center and would be monitoring the earpieces and sending messages to the group with the equipment he had brought. Gage took a deep breath, sending a surge of love over to Elliot, who took his hand, pressing a kiss to the center of his palm.

It was time to get his brother back.

26

Elliot sucked at fighting; Ian and Rolf had been trying to train him, but he wasn't the best. He knew Gage would have preferred him to stay with the helicopter, but they didn't know what other spells might be present when they got there. He was going to shift to his cat when they arrived, hoping those instincts would be better at defending himself. He had practiced sensing magic in both of his forms, so he could still help that way.

As they drove within a mile of the compound, they parked the van and climbed out. It had been packed, not meant to hold that many adults comfortably. Mates had ended up sitting on each other and others were standing bent over in the back cargo area, but at least it got them all there at the same time. Elliot moved to the other side of the vehicle, pulling off his clothes and changing to his jaguar. Gage put his clothes in the van, having already stuffed a pair of gym shorts in his cargo pants in case Elliot needed to change back. He still wasn't used to being naked around everyone.

"Everyone hear me okay?" Daryl asked over the earpieces. As everyone replied, Elliot's cat gave a rumble for his confirmation, Sam a soft woof. It looked like most of the other paranormals were going in human form. His cat rubbed against Gage, scenting his mate to calm himself. "Alright, head out. I have a drone in the air to capture heat signatures; hopefully it will be able to sense inside the compound, but at least it will help notify of someone trying to escape." Soon after, Elliot's ears twitched as he looked up and saw a small drone. He wouldn't have paid much attention if he hadn't known it was coming.

"Okay, it's in position. Good luck guys. Right now, it's picking up a few heat signatures. It looks like there might be underground cells, the heat signatures are faint. At least ten people on the main ground floor. They're wandering pretty far, so my guess would be guards."

"Be safe," Gage told him, bending down to kiss his head. Elliot licked his mate in return, getting a small smile.

There were no outside lights as they approached, which he figured made sense. If you had a secret compound, you wouldn't want any lights to draw attention to it. He scented near the hidden car, learning what Barry smelled like. He thought he caught traces of Marco, and his nose brought him to a spot in the dirt. Ian had also been tracking it, and when he crouched down to look, Elliot realized that it must be blood. He was only grateful that it didn't seem like a lot, although he was sure that Marco would have put up a fight if he was able to.

'It's Marco's blood,' Ian confirmed. *'It's no' fresh, probably when they first brought him here. The trail leads to the front door.'*

With that, Ian joined his group and they all moved into place. They had already discussed how they were splitting up before they had loaded into the van. Part of Daryl and Rick's group were taking the back entrance, along with Tess, Sam, Merri, and Duncan. The rest of the Nightwood Clan and the other part of their friends' group were going in the front. Duncan could lay down dragon fire even in human form, at least enough to stop Barry from escaping out the back. The plan was to meet in the middle and head to the lower level or levels. Thanks to Daryl's drone, they knew there was at least one.

'Ready? One. Two. Three,' Rolf said over the Clan telepathic link. The magic users in their group manipulated the locks to open the doors after ensuring that there were no alarms or traps set. It honestly seemed too easy to get in, but maybe Barry had become lax in his security, relying on the concealment and Tamer spells he had in place. To be fair, no one had found this place in hundreds of years.

The first guard was sleeping, just inside the door. Berkley quickly cast another spell to keep him that way before they restrained him. It would help if they managed to capture a few and were able to question them and have them testify to the Convocation. Rick and Daryl's group had a few witches and they had also brought sleeping potions. The goal was to rescue with the least number of lives lost, even those who they considered on the wrong side of this.

Personally, Elliot was worried about keeping Barry alive. He clearly had the means and ability to bring people to his side, either by bribery or by convincing them he was right. But they'd cross that bridge when they captured him, he guessed.

He slunk into the next room, scenting two people, trying to stay blended into the shadows until backup arrived.

'Two in here. Guards,' he said over the link.

Gage entered the room, sword in hand, a revolver on his hip.

"You're under arrest by the Convocation's order. Place your weapons down and your hands behind your back to be handcuffed," Gage ordered. Everyone who had come to help them who were in human form had been given at least one pair of Tamer spelled handcuffs.

The largest guard scoffed, pulling out a gun and pointing it at Gage. "I don't think so. I only see one of you." Elliot laughed in his head; everyone else was working their way down the hallways and clearing rooms, but they would all come running if needed. Plus, he was here. And Gage was immortal, so while it would hurt, he wouldn't die from being shot, Elliot reminded himself.

The second guard grunted in agreement before rushing Gage. Elliot's heart pounded as he watched his mate bring his sword up to stop the attack. As Gage fought off the one guard, the first one started to circle behind, trying to attack Gage's back. Elliot bared his teeth. Not on his watch, he thought to himself as his leg muscles bunched, propelling him across the room to sink his teeth into the guard's arm. He held on even as the taste of blood filled his mouth, causing his nose to wrinkle. Eww, the human part of his brain thought. As the guard raised the gun to strike Elliot's head, he wondered how he could avoid it.

"Sleep," another voice said, smashing a vial on the guard's head.

Elliot rumbled his thanks to the witch from Daryl's team. He watched as Gage restrained and gagged both guards. His man certainly was sexy when he was fighting, Elliot thought, his tail twitching. He followed them to the main hallway, stopping when they ran into the other group.

"Everything up here is clear. Guards are all restrained. Everyone ready to move to the lower level? We'll clear that floor and if there are other levels, we'll clear them one by one," Leo said as he joined them. He was only wearing a pair of gym shorts and was carrying a gun and a sword. Elliot wasn't sure where he had gotten them.

"I think they may be on to you," Daryl said suddenly in their ears. "There's movement at the bottom of the stairs, so be prepared to go in fighting. I'm still seeing heat signatures staying put, so I would guess those are the cells. There is one body running toward a room, not sure what that is, but I'll keep an eye on it. If it's Barry, you may want to get him first if you can. There's no way for me to know if he has kill-switches or anything similar set up," he warned.

Leo nodded, handing off his weapons. "I'll go in shifted; I can hide easier. I'll track Barry. If needed I can bite him and at least slow him down. I'll shift and fight hand to hand if it comes to that. I want to make sure these people are saved," he said.

Elliot understood. They hadn't come all this way to lose the chance to save these people now. He wasn't sure if Barry was the type to have a failsafe set up, but if he was collecting for his own greed, he might be the type of person to think that if he couldn't have them, then no one could. He watched as Leo shifted back to his snake, slithering away down the stairs, keeping to the shadows so he could hide better. The witches gathered at the top, holding hands, chanting. Berkley was with them, adding his magic. As they finished, pushing forward with their hands, Elliot felt the spell fly down the stairs, hitting those gathered at the bottom, causing them to drop down in a deep sleep. He let his senses open up, searching for any hidden spells lurking beneath them.

'I'm only sensing the Tamer spells at the moment,' he told the group over the Nightwood Clan link.

"Elliot says the bottom is currently clear of spells," Gage told the rest of them.

He hung back, letting the ones more experienced with fighting lead the way, but he kept sending his senses out searching for other magic and spells that could be hiding. As they passed a room that looked like a laboratory, he reached out to his family.

'There's not an active spell in this room, but I can tell it was used frequently and none of them feel pleasant. There's some dark-feeling magic that was used in there. You should be careful when you're examining it later,' he warned. They knew Barry had been trying to make himself immortal, and from the grossness

he was sensing in that room, he would guess that was where Barry did a lot of his experimenting.

Berkley nodded, attaching a red ribbon to the door, letting the rest of the team know to use caution. They weren't going to investigate the rooms until after they subdued all the guards and captured Barry, but they had been marking areas as they went. So far there had been this lab, and a kitchen and an office/guard room on the main floor. One of the witches had put a protection spell around the guards' room as it seemed to have video feed of different places in the compound. They were hoping to get more evidence to support their case. The brief glance they had of it didn't show Marco, but they were still hopeful they would find him, especially after finding some of his blood outside.

Hearing a commotion farther down the hallway, they surged forward. Elliot could sense something magic building.

'Something's going on. There's a spell being created. Be careful!' he shouted as he ran with the others. He watched as Berkley quickly erected a protective shield in front of the group. He let the magic direct him and he found himself leading them to a back room that looked like an office. He could smell Barry and Leo but didn't see them yet. Crouching down, he crept forward trying to see what was going on.

Leo was naked, fighting with Barry who was thankfully not naked but was armed. He watched in alarm as Barry grabbed a dark vial filled with an oily-looking fluid. As he continued chanting, Elliot realized what it was.

'Death spell!' he yelled. Gage cursed, running forward to knock Leo out of the way as Berkley and the witches hurriedly grabbed hands and invoked a containment spell. Just as Barry released the vial from his hands, the dome surrounded him, the glass cracking on the invisible shield, shattering within the sphere. He watched as the horror and understanding dawned on Barry's face. He tried to reach out and grab something else, but Berkley threw another spell,

freezing him in place. Elliot had to close his eyes as the death spell slowly ate away at Barry's body.

"My thanks," Leo said to Gage. Elliot looked over and quickly raised his head. He'd forgotten Leo was naked.

Elliot moved to stand next to Shaye, bumping her leg with his head. He knew she didn't want to watch Barry's death either and was worried about how her empathy was handling this.

"I'm okay," she said quietly. "Rolf is helping block it. I really want to find the prisoners though. They need my help."

'I know. Soon. I think they want to make sure Barry is dead and I'll look for any other traps he might have set. I'm not sensing any right now, but we'll need to be careful,' Elliot replied.

27

They cleared the area, finding a few captives who told them there was another layer to the compound with more guards to fight through. Some of the witches stayed behind, helping remove Tamer spells and getting started with any healing needed. As they reached the bottom floor, they could see multiple hallways shooting off in different directions from a large open room in the center. Marco was collapsed on the ground, not moving. He was chained to the floor at his wrists, ankles, and neck. Gage growled at the injuries visible on his brother. His beast was frustrated that they still couldn't sense him even though they could clearly see him. The smirking guards surrounding Marco clearly thought they had the upper hand, one of them laughing as he kicked his brother in the ribs. While his body moved, Marco didn't make a sound. That worried Gage; it was a hard kick, he should have responded in some way, even a grunt.

Suddenly Shaye ran forward, not looking at anything besides getting to Marco. Gage could tell nothing would stop her from helping his brother. Ian swore and took off after her, Elliot following to check for hidden magic. A few of the guards rushed toward her, but she dodged them, trusting that

Ian running next to her would keep her safe. He was fast, taking out the guards before they could touch her. As she dropped to her knees beside Marco, her hands hovered over his body.

"I need these cuffs off! Now!" she ordered, trying to open the wrist cuffs.

Gage grunted as a kick landed to his side. He focused back on the guards rushing out of other hallways at the commotion. As he fought them back, he saw Sam out of the corner of his eye, his wolf carrying something in his mouth that looked like a key ring. Ian took the keys from him, trying each one until he found one that fit. As the first set fell away, Gage could almost sense his brother, it was like a shadow flickering at the edge of awareness. The second pair holding his ankles together were quickly removed as well, the sensation of his brother getting closer. When the neck ring fell away, Gage almost dropped to his knees both in relief to feel his brother again and at the sudden flash of pain that transmitted through their bond. He quickly dispatched the last guard and stood watch over Shaye and Marco.

Shaye had her hands on Marco, sending her healing through him. "Berkley! There's a spell here!"

Neil followed, coming closer, watching as they worked. "Does she have magic?" he asked Gage quietly.

Despite the circumstances, Gage had to smile. "Our Shaye is a bit of an oddity like us. She was born human with a healing gift. It was horrible for her in terms of the consequences for using it, not that it ever stopped her. When she turned, it became more manageable. She's one of the ones we've protected. Not many know of her gifts." He twitched with the need to be closer to his brother but didn't want to get in Shaye's way.

Nodding, Neil went to kneel next to her. "Can I help? I have some healing and can boost you, I think," he offered. When Shaye looked back at Gage, he nodded. If the myths about phoenixes were true, he was downplaying it a bit. Rumor had it they could even reverse death. He wasn't sure on Neil's limitations though and how much of the myths were true.

"Can I link with you? I can show you where I need to focus the most," Shaye said. When Neil nodded, Rolf stood next to them, placing a hand on either shoulder. "Rolf will help with the link," she explained.

Rick came and stood next to Gage, watching over his uncle. "Hello, old friend," he greeted Gage. "I didn't know you all had a healer," he said, his tone deliberately neutral.

"I had to protect my family," Gage said simply.

When Rick nodded, Gage knew he understood and wouldn't hold Gage's withholding of Shaye's ability against him. Just like he wouldn't hold a grudge for not knowing about Neil before now. You had to protect your loved ones at any cost, even at the risk of trusted friendships.

"I'm glad Neil got to meet someone else who has a similar type of gift. He's the only healer and medical professional in our family. And he stays close to home because of his shifter side. Do you think she'd be open to talking to him? It'll give him someone to talk to about stuff we don't really get," Rick asked. His uncle had his family and some friends at home, but he knew it was hard being the only one in the family with his job.

"I'm sure. Shaye is a wonderful person. She loves having a big family, so you'll probably all be adopted in after this. She, Tess, and Doc are all in the medical field, if Neil ever needs to talk about the medical side of things as well."

It took almost half an hour, but Shaye finally sat back. Gage could tell Marco wasn't one hundred percent yet, but the broken bones and gaping wounds had been dealt with.

"He needs to rest, but he's on his way to healing. I can do more later, but I can feel others who need my help," Shaye said, looking up at Gage.

While Shaye had been working on Marco, the rest of the team had split up and worked at getting the Tamer spells removed from the other captives. He could tell she was torn between wanting to completely heal Marco and helping the others she could now sense. Gage also knew she would need to pace herself, even though she would push herself to exhaustion to help.

"I'll carry him upstairs and have someone stand guard. As we find more people, we can have them moved there so we can keep an eye on everyone. Neil can help heal and boost you, and if you need to draw on us, you let us know. If it's simply scrapes and bruises, let them go for now," Gage told her, looking her right in the eyes so she knew he meant what he was saying.

When she didn't agree right away, Elliot spoke up. "You won't be any good to the people who need help the most if you push yourself to passing out," he pointed out. "Heal the major injuries first and you can come back to help more once those are out of the way. The witches can help with the smaller injuries as well."

Shaye reluctantly nodded and she, Berkley, and Neil stood to work their way through the compound.

"From what's been reported back from the others, it's a meandering labyrinth on this level. They've marked their path with string to show which hallways have been explored so far. They're working on removing any Tamer spells and restraints, as well as stabilizing anyone who needs it. As we move people out, we'll mark the hallway entrance with an X to show it's been cleared," Gage told them. He watched as Rolf went with them to help them link together for any healing sessions. Elliot licked a kiss to his hand.

'You okay?' he asked as Gage knelt next to his brother.

"I will be when he wakes up. I know he'll be fine; Shaye wouldn't stop until he was safe." Gage breathed out a sigh, looking over his brother. Even with the major injuries healing or healed, he could still see bruises and contusions all over his body. He must have put up one heck of a fight. "You should go with them, make sure there aren't any booby traps. I'll bring him upstairs and see if I can't collect some blankets and pillows from somewhere. Barry didn't seem like the type to go without his own comforts, plus the guards must have had some as well." Gage slipped the Nightwood Clan pendant over Marco's head, relaxing a little with the knowledge that there was a magical layer of protection over him.

Elliot nodded, giving his mate one last lick before following Shaye's group down the first hallway.

Daryl had informed them over the headsets that he had sent a coded request to Rob's contact at the Convocation and Leo's boss to ask for medical assistance. Leo was part of a paranormal branch of the federal agencies, and they would be better equipped to help the people they found. Leo had already cleared everyone they were calling in for help ahead of time; he had a TruthSpeaker ability as well, so he had been able to make sure they weren't working with Barry. Gage picked up his brother, wondering if anyone had told Gawain he could come down and that there would be additional incoming. He figured he better let him know just in case.

28

Elliot guzzled down the bottle of water, thirsty after traipsing through what seemed to be miles of hallways. They had found over one hundred people, some of them the children from the breeding camps. From what he understood from Gage, there had been one or two of the rare paranormals, but most had been ones that were more limited in numbers or had special powers. He had been surprised to learn there were a few unicorns, as well as the Sabre family that had been neighbors to Daryl's aunt. The children of course were now grown, but at least they would have a chance to live a normal-ish life again.

Daryl had contacted his family and someone was coming to bring the Sabres home. Daryl himself was still out in the van, not trusting the other government aid even with Leo clearing them. Elliot couldn't blame him; he had seen what happened when someone in power went bad. Who was to say that it wouldn't happen again? That's why their group had all met quickly and decided to not mention Neil's or Shaye's abilities. They were keeping all talk about shifter sides quiet, not wanting anyone to find out what Gage or Doc were. All mention of or talking to Doc was done over the Clan links, as they weren't sure if the unicorns would recognize him. Neil kept his concealment watch on. There were a few other humans, including Rick in their group, so he didn't stand out too much.

Once the building had been cleared of any magical traps, Elliot had gone back to help on the main floor, which was filled to capacity. They'd had no idea how many people were being held and had brought them to the cafeteria, which was the largest room. Eventually, they realized that they didn't have anywhere near enough space. It was almost claustrophobic with how crowded it was, but they didn't want to force people back to the holding cell levels. Instead, they had made do and expanded into the hallways and other rooms on the main floor. They opened any windows, made sure all internal doors were left open. The last thing they wanted was to make people feel trapped again.

The noise was making his cat twitchy; he needed to be close to his mate, to hold him for a second. He figured he was more help now as a man anyway, as he would have hands. His cat was awesome, but not that great at helping injured people. He moved off to a side room where someone had gathered extra supplies. He grabbed a pair of flip flops in his teeth and searched out his mate to get his shorts. There had been some in the storage room, but his nose wrinkled at the thought of putting on someone else's shorts when he didn't have underwear.

Elliot quickly changed, grabbing Gage into a hard hug. He felt himself settle down as he felt strong arms surround him. He drew in a breath and let the scent of his mate flow through him. He could still smell the base of Gage even under the smells of dust, gunpowder, and the metallic tang of blood. Gage held on until Elliot pressed a soft kiss to his lips and stepped back.

"Thank you. I needed just a second to hold you," Elliot explained.

"I'm always up for a hug," Gage reassured him. "I needed one too. This experience is horrifying. I know people can do awful things; I've seen it. But this...this is hitting me hard." Leo called Gage's name and he gave Elliot another kiss, squeezing his hand, before walking over to consult. Elliot took a deep breath, feeling a tendril of Shaye's calming swirl around him through the Clan link. He found a small smile and walked around to see if there was someone who needed help that he could provide. He couldn't do much, but he could grab blankets and waters.

The sound of sniffles and quiet whispers caught his attention and his cat urged him to find the source. A few minutes later, he stumbled upon a small group of teenagers huddled in the corner. There was a mix of ages and genders, but they were all huddled so close together, there was barely any space between them. They were holding hands or touching each other in some way, arms linked, a hand on a knee, legs pressed against each other. Their heads close together, several of them crying, others trying to reassure them.

"I just want to go home," one of the younger girls said brokenly. "I won't even complain about going back to school and doing my homework."

It wasn't a funny situation but that made his lips quirk up a little bit. His cat kept pushing him to go over and something in his brain finally clicked and he remembered the missing kids from his hometown. As he walked over, he made sure they saw him coming so he wouldn't spook them.

"Can I get you guys anything? Water? Blankets? I know this is going to sound weird but are you from Rivenpoint?" he asked.

The kids looked at each other, but no one answered.

"My dad is Steven. And you might know my cousin Baz? He's here as well. Let me call him over." Elliot looked around and saw Baz across the room. He shouted for him, although it took three tries before Baz looked his way. As he waved him over, one of the kids finally spoke.

"I didn't think Mr. Steven had a…um, I thought you were all vampires?" the boy asked cautiously.

"I was human, but I recently changed," Elliot told them.

"Oh! You're Elliot," another girl said.

He looked at the kids again, convinced Baz was now making his way over to them.

"I am," he replied.

"Can you help us call our parents? I really want my mom," the youngest girl asked.

He hoped Baz had his phone because his was currently sitting in his pants in the van. Shaye walked by, her eyes roaming over the room. As soon as she saw him, she weaved her way through the crowd. Elliot could feel the calming vibes she was pushing out as she got closer. The kids slowly relaxed, not looking quite as scared.

"Hey, thanks. Can I borrow your phone? Mine's in the van. I need to call my dad and let him know we found the kids from my hometown. He needs to let the parents know where to come," Elliot asked.

"Yeah, of course!" She handed over the phone to Elliot before crouching down in front of the kids. "Hey. My name is Shaye and I've been friends with Elliot for a long time. I'm part of the Nightwood Clan. Can I sit with you for a minute?"

As they nodded their heads, she sat, gently asking them questions, all the while keeping them calm. Elliot quickly dialed his dad, one ear listening as Shaye unobtrusively made sure the kids weren't hurt and hadn't been experimented on or spelled.

"Dad, hey. We found them, including the kids from home. I can't talk long, we're still sorting and helping people, but I wanted to let you know. This is Shaye's phone, I don't have mine right now. I'm sending you the location of where we are so you can get the parents mobilized. The kids seem shaken, but not hurt. I think Baz has his phone, so you can call him too," Elliot said.

"You're okay?" his dad asked.

"I am, didn't get a scratch on me," Elliot reassured him.

"Okay. Good. Send it to me and I'll get things started here. Hopefully we can get there today. I'll text him, but if you see Baz first, ask him to keep an eye on the kids and to keep them together."

"Will do."

As they hung up, he looked up and saw Baz standing there.

"Hey. I thought the kids might recognize you. I already called Dad and let him know we found them. He's contacting the parents. I don't have my phone, so I told him to contact you or Shaye if he needed to reach us."

Baz nodded. "I have it on me. I'll sit here for a bit and let them call home. Shout if you need me."

As Baz sat down with the kids, he heard Shaye say goodbye and she made her way over to him.

"You okay?" she asked.

"Yeah. How are you holding up? Make sure you don't overdo it," he cautioned.

"I'm good," she said, giving him a quick side hug before walking to the next set of people. He knew his friend though; she was totally going to push herself as far as she could to help these people.

Shaye and Neil looked exhausted, but at least everyone who had any major injuries or infections were taken care of. Rolf and Rick were standing guard over the pair, making sure they got water and food, looking formidable enough that no one tried to get past them to the healers. Gawain and Duncan had flown to the nearest town, grabbing take-out food and flying it back. It must be nice to be a flying shifter and not have to worry about having clothes when you change, Elliot thought a little enviously. As nice as that was though, he still wouldn't have picked anything different.

He kept an eye on Shaye as she snuck over to Marco. He saw Rolf watching her out of the corner of his eye, so she hadn't been as sneaky as she thought.

"Aren't you supposed to be taking a break?" Elliot asked her, making her startle.

"Um. I did, ate and everything," she said, aiming for an innocent look.

Elliot snorted. "Uh huh."

"I wanted to check on Marco. He should have woken up by now," she said worriedly, sitting down next to him.

"I'm up, just don't want to people," Marco grumbled.

"You jerk, I was worried," Shaye exclaimed, poking him gently.

Marco grunted, but gave a slight smile, keeping his eyes closed.

"How do you feel?" Shaye asked, running a hand over him.

"Sore as fuck. Thanks for helping with the broken stuff. Don't push yourself, the rest will get there. The major issues are fixed," Marco told her quietly.

Elliot caught Gage's attention, nodding him over.

"Glad to see you awake, brother. I missed you," Gage said, sitting down by Marco's head.

"Me too," Marco replied simply, but his hand reached out, grabbing Gage's.

"How'd they get you?" Gage asked.

"Trap. One of the locations I was given was a trap. He had more guards there than I could fight off. They shot me with something, it must have been a Tamer spell because I shifted back to human and fell right out of the sky. When I wouldn't give him any information on how close we were to finding him, he tried torturing it out of me.

"From what I overheard, our guesses were correct. Barry was trying to both build himself an army and to make himself immortal. He was experimenting with bonds and tried breaking the one I have to you. Luckily, he had no idea what it was, just that I had a tie to another person. He was very frustrated when it wouldn't break. I guess he thought that if he broke bonds between people that they would be more willing to bond with him? Or he could force them to bond to him? I don't know, it didn't make much sense to me. He made several comments that made me think I was the only one here with one that wasn't a mate bond. He spent a lot of time with different potions, spells, and even a few poisons to try to break it. I think he was just willing to try anything," Marco said.

"It wouldn't work," Shaye said quietly. "We've seen that the mate and Clan bonds are protected. They're warded against interference. It was how we were able to save Sam; using the bonds to push back against the death spell. I think Fate must have made our kind of bonds protected, warded bonds, if you will."

"That makes sense," Marco said. "Nothing he did worked. Can you imagine the chaos if those bonds could be broken by an outsider? Did you find the others?"

Gage nodded, even though Marco couldn't see him. "Yeah. We've rounded everyone up and made this level the headquarters of sorts. We have several teams working through the building and collecting any evidence. Gawain and Merri are one of the teams trying to sort through everything, so we've been getting good updates. It's a mess.

"Some of these people haven't ever seen the real world, some haven't seen it in hundreds of years. We're going to have to train a lot of them on how to exist in the modern world, create new identities for some of them. I'm glad I'm only helping and not in charge of all of it," Gage added.

Marco nodded, but his body was still healing and he drifted back to sleep quickly.

Gage looked at Shaye, wanting to make sure Marco was okay. His shoulders dropped in relief when she nodded.

"He's just tired. Healing takes a lot of effort on a body, even with Neil and me helping it along," she said.

Elliot joined the Nightwood Clan in the guards' office several days later. Gawain had called a family meeting; he had found something and wanted to let the rest of them know before he gave it to the official investigators. While they trusted a lot of the people here, they were still using a lot of caution. Barry sympathizers were still being tracked down and the Convocation was in a vulnerable position as it cleaned house. Their family was only fully trusting each other; they had too many unique gifts that would be valuable to someone who wanted to exploit them. They had a video call set up so Marge, Emma, and Doc could participate. Berkley was currently casting a silencing dome over the room.

Among the many questions that needed answers, Merri and Gawain had been trying to find answers to a few specific ones: what happened to the "regular" kids from the breeding camps, why Barry would kill the breeding camps but not the people in this building when he was cleaning up his tracks. And who the dead body was.

While most of the people had been found alive in their cells, they had found a graveyard of sorts in the compound. They had also found the remains of a body in an old cell far away from everyone else. It had scented heavily of Barry, although none of the other captives had known who the deceased was.

"The body is his father," Gawain said sadly once Berkley gave him a nod the room was safe. "I found a diary of sorts in the office. His father did have a trancing ability, one that was extremely strong. As he got older, Barry realized he himself didn't have any special skills, something that disappointed his father, and made Barry feel inadequate. Reading his logs, he slowly got more paranoid that his father would use the ability on him. No real reason was listed for his belief, just a lot of ramblings. He clearly felt lacking.

"He wanted to get the upper hand somehow, convinced that he needed power behind him since he didn't have anything special. He had a plan. Not a good one, but a plan. Barry tried to convince his father to breed in an attempt to pass on the trancing ability. His father didn't agree with the breeding plan for himself; it's not clear whether it was because he realized his son was crazy, it didn't match his own idea for the future, or something else.

"He goes into detail early on about how he planned to wait until any offspring were born to imprison his father. Once his father was out of the way—no mention of the mother at all— Barry planned to raise any offspring as his own. He thought he could mold them and control them for his own benefit. Barry wrote his father refused to consider anyone who wasn't a vampire but turned down everyone Barry brought to him. He grew frustrated by his father's lack of cooperation and changed the plan, locking him up. He doesn't mention how he managed to do that though. Barry thought once he had his father contained, that he would give in to Barry's demands. He didn't. When simple imprisonment didn't work, Barry started withholding food and blood. From the log, it appears his father died of malnutrition, as he never accepted a forced mating.

"When he was unsuccessful with his father, he turned his attention to his own version of a breeding program. He even tried mating with a few of the females himself. His notes show that he was livid that he never produced a child of his own."

"That's kind of fucked up," Sam said. "The whole thing is, but he even imprisoned his only family and tried a forced breeding program on him?"

"It's good for us though. Crazy might have run through those genes, and we definitely don't need another Barry or his father creating havoc on the paranormal community. This is going to be a big enough mess to clean up," Gage said.

"Merri found a logbook. We took pictures of it as well. Barry was definitely the reason there has been a resurgence in hunters. Between that and the diary, we know how he was recruiting. For humans, he went for the religious fanatics. Not the everyday religious type of person, but the kind who are zealots, who believe in possessions and demons and are fearful of anything they can't explain. He fostered that fear and hate and trained them a bit in killing paranormals, telling them they all worked for Satan. He had a witch he worked with create the pendants to detect paranormals.

"Barry paid his paranormal hunters quite a lot. Some of them were Vlad sympathizers, joining so they could take down non-vampires. Others were like the witch who attacked Sam, rogues who only cared about themselves and money. Barry would go around to different online groups or even in-person events and recruit," Gawain told them. "For as much as Barry's journal was scatter-brained, his blackmail and recordkeeping log was on point. He listed names, aliases, had pictures, descriptions, and locations. Leo has already sent someone to hunt them down."

"Any evidence of who his other inside contact was?" Gage asked.

"Remember our unwanted visitor?" Merri asked.

"The lady from the Convocation?" Sam asked.

She nodded. "She's cleared; even though she's a bitch, she wasn't involved. Her TruthSpeaker however, was. He's been working with Barry, sending him information he found. He was able to create a fake Convocation email account and make it look like it came from a real Convocation member, which was what he used to request Marco. The diary spells out the whole plan and Daryl has traced it back and confirmed."

"Oh! And not that it matters as much since Barry's dead, but the Roanoke archeologist reached out last night," Gawain added. "He had been out of the country and didn't have cell phone reception. He was still hesitant to share contact information with any other descendants that I hadn't spoken to already but did confirm he had family from the Roanoke settlement. A journal had been passed down, detailing the disappearances. They had everyone willing to write of the event add their own story to the book. One person had survived being attacked; they wrote about being paralyzed and not able to call out for help, but their mate had sensed it and had come running with a group of others.

"When their attacker ran away, the paralysis disappeared. So, while it does confirm the father's ability, it seems like he needed to be close to his victims to use it. There were other accounts of the colonists witnessing two people dragging someone away. One of the journalists was a talented artist and sketched out the attackers. One of the sketches matches Barry and the other matches the photograph of what we believe is Barry's father from his office," Gawain reported.

"Do we know what's happening with the victims yet?" Shaye asked. She had been going through daily, helping everyone heal. Neil had been such a big help, and she was looking forward to talking to him about his own healing ability when they weren't in the midst of everything. She thought he seemed a bit lonely, even with his huge family. She had Tess and Doc to talk medical stuff with at least, and she would happily share them with Neil.

"The Convocation is doing a deep clean and has ferreted out a few more Barry sympathizers, especially after finding some email and paper trails thanks to Daryl and Rick's contact," Gage spoke up. "It doesn't matter if they were blackmailed, they had the opportunity to say something. They're all gone and there are a few spots that are now left open on the Convocation. I don't know what they're going to do with those yet.

"They have set up training programs for the ones who have been captive the longest; daily life type of things like banking, driving, laundry machines, and computers, as well as history classes. Of course, some of them may not want to interact with anyone ever again. I can't say I blame them if they take to the woods and become hermits, but at least they'll have more useable skills if they need them. I think they're going to ask if some of the easier ones can come to Rockfort," Gage added, looking at Rolf. He was the Sheriff for the town and the Warden for the area, but the town was really Rolf's. He wasn't going to say yes or no to an official Convocation request when it came without talking to Rolf first.

Rolf looked around at his family. "I think it would be on a per-person or family basis," he said slowly, clearly thinking. "Rockfort is meant to be a safe haven for paranormals and humans. The wards will keep ill-intentioned people out, but that doesn't mean that an asshole or someone who is bigoted couldn't make it through and cause problems. I think we would need to review and discuss each case before we said yes. I would love to help everyone in need, but I have to think of the town first. We've worked so hard at making it a safe place for everyone, and I don't want to put that in jeopardy. So yes, I'm willing to help but we need to have final say in who it is."

Gage nodded. It made perfect sense to him. If they had someone who hated humans, or even same sex couples, while they may not cause physical harm, there was still emotional harm or disrupting the vibe the town now had. He wasn't naïve enough to think that Rockfort was some utopia, but it was a darn good place to live, and they all had worked hard to make that happen.

"I agree. It might not be a bad idea to have an empath or a TruthSpeaker sit in on any interviews," Gage replied. He knew firsthand just how good some people were at lying.

"Or at least have something spelled to indicate lies or untruthfulness," Tess offered.

"We have a lot of connections in town that could help with teaching job skills," Sam added thoughtfully. "We really could help a lot of people get their feet under them and the town is a great place to show that not everyone is an asshole."

"What happened to the regular children from the breeding camps?" Marge asked. "I'm not sure I want to know, but I think I need to know so I'm not always wondering."

"Is Jimmy there?" Merri asked.

"No. He's in his room playing video games. I'm outside," Marge replied.

Merri let out a deep sigh and Elliot knew right then that it wasn't good news. "We still don't know everything, but from what we can put together from a lot of different notes and logs, it's a mixed bag. I think he let some of them go, those who were deemed weak and wouldn't pose a threat. Especially the really young children who wouldn't remember anything as they aged. Those labeled as leader quality, strong-willed, or who were old enough to retain childhood memories, they…" she broke off, shaking her head.

"Barry left a trail of unmarked graveyards across the country," Gawain said. "We're mapping where they are so these children won't be forgotten."

There was a long moment of silence; everyone had suspected they might be dead, but the confirmation was still horrific. Elliot had a hard time imagining how someone could become such a monster as to kill innocent children.

"God. That's…I don't understand why he would…" Marge muttered, her voice thick. Elliot thought she was holding back tears.

"He wasn't stable in the slightest. The breeding camps were deemed not worth saving, as they were mostly experiments on getting the traits he desired. He picked people for their gifts and traits that ran in their families, hoping that different pairings would give him what he wanted. He moved a few here, ones he thought had the most potential, but most were killed to cleanse the trail behind him. I believe Leo's group is going to arrest and prosecute those remaining ones; after all they willingly participated and agreed to sell any child they might have," Gawain said. "They are also trying to track down any who were released; they want to make sure they don't have any spells lingering that could harm them later. This whole thing is a mess and awful."

Elliot couldn't agree more.

30

A knock on the doorframe had Elliot looking up from rolling out cookies. Gage stood there, out of uniform, Emma standing behind him grinning like crazy.

"Hey! I thought you had work today," Elliot said, walking over to give his mate a kiss. He held his arms away from his body so he didn't get any flour or goop on Gage.

"I did, but I decided we've been working way too much lately and haven't had enough us time," Gage said.

Elliot nodded. They had been rather busy. Between him taking over the bakery, the whole Barry thing, and Gage helping transition the kidnapped paranormals, they had been lucky to spend any time together. Thank goodness for telepathy or some days they wouldn't even have been able to talk to each other. "It's been a little busy, but it should settle down soon." He hoped; Gage was still working crazy hours with the newcomers and dealing with the Convocation.

After they had launched the rescue, it had still ended up taking a couple of weeks before everyone in the family arrived back home to Rockfort for good. Marco had left the day after the rescue, saying he was strong enough to teleport himself home. That had been a fight, and really the first time he had seen Gage and Marco yell at each other. Gage had wanted to keep Marco close so he could watch over him. Marco was overwhelmed with the amount of people and wanted to be by himself. The compromise the brothers had settled on was that Marco would go to the Nightwood Clan home to finish healing. Doc and Emma had kept an eye on him, making sure he rested and ate as he healed. Gage had told him that Marco had been worried about pulling Shaye's attention from those who needed her more. It took him a few days to finish healing, but he was completely better now.

Once Shaye had healed everyone with major injuries, she and Rolf went home. They hadn't wanted to draw more attention to Shaye. Neil and Daryl had also left as soon as the major crisis was out of the way. For the rest of them, there had been reports to take, sorting to do, trying to figure out the best path to help these people. Some had been captive their whole lives. They needed education and training on how to exist in the real world. Rolf had also begun work to get things set up in Rockfort to handle the people who would be sent there.

Elliot had stayed with Gage for a week or so, but once they started moving people either into new homes and identities or to training centers to bring them up to speed on modern life, he hadn't had much to do and had gone back to Rockfort. He had a feeling the Convocation didn't want many "outsiders" there anyway. He had been so relieved when Gage had finally said enough and came back home. He still was on the phone all day and had tons of paperwork to do, but at least he was home.

"I can't take long," Gage started saying, bringing Elliot's attention back to the present. There was an apology in his voice as he continued, "but I feel like our mating needs"— Elliot's heart about stopped, waiting for something horrible to happen. He knew they were pretty solid, but so much had happened since they had met, "—some time to itself. I booked a hotel room for us and we're going on a weekend trip.

Emma's taking over for the rest of the day and the rest of the Clan are helping while we're away," Gage finished.

"Really?" Elliot asked, his heart racing now for a different reason. Besides coming to Rockfort and searching for Marco, he still hadn't been many places.

Gage grinned as he pulled out a travel bag from behind the doorframe. "Really. Not too far, Charleston. But we can drive there tonight and have a day or two to ourselves. It overlooks the harbor. It's walking distance to a lot of things."

Elliot bounced on his toes. Holy crap this was the best surprise. He looked at Emma. "And you're okay with this?" he asked. He wanted to make sure she wasn't going to be overwhelmed.

Emma nodded. "Yes," she said firmly. "Go wash up and get out of here. Take lots of pictures. I've never been there."

Elliot grinned, running to the sink. He grabbed Emma in a hug once he was clean. "Thank you!"

He reached out, grabbing Gage by the belt and pulling him in close for a kiss. "Thank you. This is a wonderful surprise."

Gage laughed. "We aren't even there yet," he protested.

"It's the thought," Elliot replied. Even if it rained the entire time they were gone, his lover had made the effort to make a romantic getaway for them.

The drive went quickly as they were able to simply hold hands and talk, no phones ringing and interrupting. Gage had packed drinks and snacks in a cooler in the back seat of the SUV, making sure Elliot had all of his favorites. As they pulled up to the hotel, Elliot stared at the hotel building. The front was okay, nothing terribly special; maybe four stories high, made of brick and stone with metal railings along the windows. What made it spectacular was the location. It sat on a corner, cattycorner to a fountain, and farther beyond that a pier. He could see cargo boats and cruise ships in the distance.

Inside is where it really shone. There was a gleaming

wood staircase curving from the lobby to upstairs. He waited while Gage checked in and they made their way to their room. Gage opened the door, ushering him in. Elliot's breath caught as he walked inside. There was a large bed, perfect for both of them, a television of course, a gas fireplace, a small table and set of chairs, plus another sitting chair. But what really caught his attention was the gorgeous view from the balcony. It overlooked the water and there were even chairs out there to sit in. It looked so inviting.

"What do you want to do first?" Gage asked, dropping the bag, coming up to wrap his arms around him from behind.

Elliot drew in a deep breath, taking in the cinnamon roll scent of his mate. Leaning his head back to rest on his partner's shoulder, he could feel himself fully relax. He hadn't thought he'd still been tense, but being here with the quiet and the view, he realized he had still been holding on to the stress of before. He slid his hands over Gage's larger ones, content to simply stand there and look at the water. A few boats moved through their view, coming and going, the sounds from outside muffled.

A few moments later, he felt Gage's cock stir against his lower back, the heat of it sinking into his body, making his own take notice.

"How about we test out the bed first, maybe a quick nap and then find some dinner?" Elliot asked, grinding back into Gage lightly.

"Hmm...I like that idea," Gage replied, kissing his way down Elliot's ear to his neck, his hands unbuckling the belt and dropping his pants and underwear to the floor.

Elliot started panting softly as Gage's warm hands closed around his cock. He had been at half chub but as soon as Gage touched him, his penis sprang up so fast he was a bit dizzy. He swallowed his very unmanly-like scream as Gage suddenly picked him up in a bridal carry and tossed him on the bed. His eyes followed his lover as he stood at the edge of the bed ripping his own clothes off. He suppressed a giggle as Gage stumbled from forgetting he still had shoes on when he tried to step out of his pants.

"I saw that, mate," Gage rumbled, leaning over Elliot. Those perfect nubs were right there, already hard for him. Lunging up, Elliot gently bit Gage's left nipple, smiling around it as he heard Gage grunt. He quickly moved to give the other one the same attention, sliding his hands down to grab Gage's shaft, slowly dragging his hand up and down, giving his lover just enough friction to drive him crazy but not enough to make him come. He had learned what made Gage tick and he loved finding new hot spots on him. Reaching a little farther, he circled Gage's balls, rubbing his taint every few passes. Listening to the changes in Gage's breathing, Elliot tightened his grasp just a tiny bit, loving how he could make his partner feel good.

His hand was suddenly empty as Gage pulled back, dropping down to his knees. He grabbed Elliot under his ass, pulling him forward to swallow him whole. Elliot groaned as his cock was suddenly engulfed in warm wet heat, Gage's throat swallowing around him. He was lost in the sensations when he felt a finger lightly circle his hole. Spreading his legs, he tried to give Gage access to the rest of his body. As he felt something else slide against his shaft, he looked down, whimpering at the sight. Gage slid his finger out of his own mouth, now glistening wet before tapping it against Elliot's entrance. He kept his legs wide, tilting his hips up in a nonverbal plea, moaning as Gage slowly slid a finger inside him. At first Gage teasingly thrust, short and shallow mixed with long and hard, before finally pressing against Elliot's prostate.

'Please, love. I need you inside me. Now,' Elliot pleaded. He needed to feel Gage in him and all around him.

Gage stood, grabbing the suitcase and pulling out the dopp kit. He dumped the whole thing out on the nightstand before hurriedly grabbing the lube. Elliot watched hungrily as

Gage coated his dick before stepping between his thighs. As soon as he was close enough, Elliot wrapped his legs around Gage's waist, pulling him in. Gage leaned over Elliot, one hand braced on the bed near his head, his eyes staring at him, lust and love both there for him to see. Feeling the brush of knuckles, Elliot looked down, the sight of Gage guiding his cock into his body sending a flash of heat through him. They both moaned when Gage was fully seated.

Gage's breath was ragged as he waited for Elliot's body to adjust. As soon as he tightened his legs around him, Gage pulled back, almost to the point of completely disengaging. Elliot's breath stuttered as Gage plowed back into him, giving him all of the ferocity of his beast. Now that Elliot had changed, Gage had been more willing to loosen the tight grip on his control when they were together, and he loved it. Elliot drove his hips up, meeting Gage thrust for thrust, their bodies glistening with their efforts. As he felt his climax barrel closer, Gage lifted his hips and pegged his prostate dead on. He screamed out his orgasm, burying his mouth against Gage's shoulder, his teeth grabbing the salty flesh to muffle his sounds. Gage grunted, filling Elliot with his own release, gripping his hips tight.

As Elliot drifted on the orgasm high, Gage gently pulled out of his body and ran to the bathroom for a warm washcloth. Rolling his head to track his lover through barely open eyes, he frowned as he noticed something red on the bedcover. He hoped he hadn't scratched Gage. Forcing his eyes to focus, he realized he was lying on scattered flower petals.

"I wanted it to be special and they always show this in the movies," Gage admitted sheepishly, carefully cleaning him up.

"I think that's very sweet. Thank you. Now come here and snuggle," Elliot said, his heart happy, arms reaching out for his mate. Gage settled around him, curled up around his back, arm across his waist. Elliot smiled drowsily as he felt Gage kiss the back of his head, the feel of his breath and heartbeat making him feel safe.

Elliot munched on a pastry as they finished packing up. Gage had ordered room service this morning and they had made a bit of a mess on the bed with the maple syrup. It had been such a nice weekend; he hoped they could do more of these little trips. He didn't need some great big crazy vacation, and he knew Gage's work made it harder to get longer time away, but trips like this were perfect.

Yesterday had been incredible but exhausting. They had woken up early and grabbed coffee from the hotel and wandered through the town. They walked all over, and he had been pleasantly tired by the time they made it back. They had gone to Waterfront Park and taken a selfie in front of the pineapple fountain, admired the houses on Rainbow Row, shopped at the City Market (he was excited to give out the trinkets he had found to the family when they got home), and explored the Old Exchange & Provost Dungeon. He had eaten pralines, enjoyed the barbeque, and sweet tea.

The architecture was amazing and there were so many beautiful homes and buildings in the city. He hoped they could go back and take a historical tour one day, maybe venture further down south to Savannah. When they had gotten back to the hotel, they had stayed up late, taking advantage of their last night together before they got back to the real world. Not all of his muscle aches this morning were from walking, he contemplated with a grin.

"I don't know if I want to go back," Gage groused, wrapping him in a hug.

Elliot laughed, although he kind of agreed. He knew he would miss his bakery and their family though.

"You know you'd miss everyone. Shaye told me they moved back dinner and Inebriated Inconsistencies in case we made it, but no pressure to hurry home. I think they just wanted it to be fun coming home," Elliot told him.

"We might miss dinner, but should make it for the other. Marco will be happy to attend; he was so mad that his kidnapping interfered with his first attendance," Gage replied with a smile. He leaned down, pressing a kiss to Elliot's lips. "Alright, I guess we'll go home."

Elliot gave him another kiss, grabbing his hand as they walked out the door.

EPILOGUE

Elliot looked around the patio, taking in the mix of both his families. It had taken a long time to get here, it seemed, but they were finally having a quiet night with everyone present. The late January air was crisp with the threat of snow, but the backyard was nice and warm thanks to the fireplace and the magical dome Berkley had made. Elliot took a sip of his drink, relaxing back in his chair. He thought back over the past many weeks and marveled at what was now his life.

Things were finally starting to really settle down and get back to normal. They had managed to have Christmas together, but it had felt like it was squeezed in with everything else. Elliot fully believed that they had all appreciated spending the time together even more than usual. They had still been in the midst of the rescue chaos and had been juggling too much, the stress strong. Everyone had made a point to be together for Christmas day, although many of them had gone back to help at the compound the next day. It had been into January before everyone was back home to stay.

In total, the Convocation had sent about thirty people to

Rockfort. The small hotel had filled quickly, and they ended up putting a few families in rental homes. There had been an emergency fund set up to financially help those that Barry had taken. His own bank accounts had funded it, which Elliot thought was appropriate. It had taken a bit to set up accounts for everyone, but as soon as the money and IDs had come through, about half of the people had left. They had been the ones who hadn't needed as much care as they hadn't been held captive as long. The rest had decided to stay and were working on figuring out their next steps.

Rolf had been busy once he got back home setting up training programs and internships at different businesses in town. The rescued people had the option to shadow at different places to see if they would be interested in learning new skills. A few had signed up for online adult education classes that Marge and Emma helped run from a conference room in the library. Gage had been a little shocked when Emma had volunteered to work with so many strangers, but she said she knew what it was like to be under the oppression of someone else and wanted to help. Elliot even had a couple of part-timers who were helping at the bakery; it felt nice to be able to teach someone a useable skill and he hoped he would be able to do it again in the future.

Gage had been kept busy with integrating the new people into town and getting them settled. He was ultimately in charge of paperwork and the program, even though Rolf had really set it up with the townspeople. Rolf didn't work for the Convocation, and after the Barry debacle, they had been trying to keep everything very by-the-book going forward. Elliot could feel Gage's frustration at all the red tape and the papers in triplicate, not to mention having to mediate a few cultural differences between the townspeople and the rescues. Even with them being prescreened, it had been a difficult adjustment with a few of them.

Their weekend trip had been wonderful and amazing and

such a glorious surprise. They had both been able to fully relax and breathe. Coming back was a bit rough though. He had returned to his bakery and Gage had returned to a small mountain of paperwork on his desk from the Convocation. Elliot wasn't sure how that much had accumulated in just a weekend. It had turned into long hours again, and Elliot had forcibly encouraged Gage to take the next couple of hours off. He was just glad that his mate was sitting back and enjoying a beer, although he still had a frowny face on. Elliot knew he was thinking about all the work waiting for him.

"You know what? I'm just going to ban anyone leaving town from November until January," Gage threatened suddenly. "That way we won't have any more problems. The fight with Vlad, Sam and Tess's attack, Marco's kidnapping. They all happened during that time frame."

"Ian was hurt in February," Sam pointed out helpfully, a mischievous twinkle in his eyes.

"Fine. November to February everyone has to stay here. Then we'll all be safe," Gage declared grumpily. He was tired of his family being hurt. This whole thing had made his head and heart ache. Not to mention the mountains of paperwork he was still working his way through. He took some comfort that Marco lived in his town now, so he wouldn't have to worry about him being safe, at least not while he was home. When he went back to work, he would now have the protective pendant.

Marco had taken a long vacation after his ordeal and had used it to house hunt and relax. For as much as he had protested that he wanted to be alone, he had stayed at the Nightwood Clan home for most of that time and had soaked in the atmosphere there. He didn't always talk, sometimes just sat and listened to everyone, but Gage could tell it was healing something in his brother.

Marco had found a house on the outskirts of Rockfort, and

they helped him move in a few days ago. They had all been shocked when he'd been offered one of the open Convocation seats. Marco had called a family meeting, wanting to get everyone's advice. Afterward, he had reluctantly agreed to the position, but told the rest of the governing body he had a few things that were non-negotiable. Two of the biggest ones were him living in Rockfort and that Gage was not to be moved from his position there either. There were still a couple of empty seats, but no one knew who was going to fill them.

Right after they got Marco settled in, Elliot's family had descended on the town. He had been good about keeping them informed but they (aka his mother) had finally had enough, and his mom, dad, and aunt had stormed the town. They were staying in the bed and breakfast, which Gage secretly thought was best for everyone. He had enjoyed meeting more of his mate's family, but his mother was… whoa. She clearly loved Elliot, and wanted the best for him, but was a little overbearing.

Elliot had been thrilled when Baz had stuck around after the rescue, helping bring and settle people in town. Baz had gotten to know everyone in the Nightwood Clan during the rescue process and Elliot thought it had helped make the introductions between his two families a little easier.

Rolf had invited Elliot's family over for a barbeque today and he was happy to see both sides of his family getting along really well. Ian and Berkley were currently in a bean bag toss competition with Baz and his mother. Emma and his aunt were talking, sharing stories about having visions. Jimmy was having the time of his life with more people to play games with. Rockefeller wasn't quite sure what to make of all the people and he stuck close to Emma.

As he got up to grab another drink, Elliot looked at all his loved ones interacting and laughing, eating all the delicious foods, exchanging stories. Gage came up behind him, wrapping his arms around his waist, pressing a kiss to the top of his head.

He couldn't wait to see what the future held.

NOTE FROM THE AUTHOR

Thank you for reading *Warded Bond*! If you enjoyed the story, please consider leaving a review. Reviews, no matter how short, are invaluable to independent authors.

If you keep flipping through, you'll find the list of characters mentioned in the books.

I hope you've enjoyed the Nightwood Clan series. I had so much fun writing them. Although this is officially the end of the Nightwood Clan series, I don't know that I'm quite ready to say goodbye forever yet. There may be some more Nightwood Clan series in the future, things like holiday books or short stories, but the main storyline in the series is concluded in this book. Thank you for taking this journey with me!

I used Roanoke in the story as a possible paranormal colony. Of course, most people in the USA have heard of the Lost Colony in school. "CROATOAN" was carved into a post of the settlement, but there were no signs of struggle. It remains a bit of a mystery. Some people think that they had a skirmish with the native people and were killed, others think they went to the Croatoan island and lived with the friendlier natives there. There is some evidence that this might have happened. Other than the time period and the Roanoke and Croatoan names, I imagined the rest.

NIGHTWOOD CLAN

LOCATION

The series is mainly set in Rockfort, Tennessee, a fictional town next to the Great Smoky Mountains National Park.

CHARACTERS

Rolf (Rolfston)
Species: Vampire
Mate: Shaye
Job: Investments, day trading, Clan leader
Special Abilities: Telepathy, shielding
Book: Bite Me Again

Shaye
Species: Human/Vampire
Mate: Rolf
Job: Nurse
Special Abilities: Healing
Book: Bite Me Again

Sam

Species: Werewolf
Mate: Tess
Job: Brewer/Chef/Owner, Black Wolf Brewery
Rolf's friend
Book: A Hairy Situation

Tess

Species: Witch
Mate: Sam
Job: Medical coder, nurse
Shaye's friend
Book: A Hairy Situation

Emma (Emmaline)

Species: Vampire
Mate: Doc (Albert)
Job: Landowner/small farm
Special Abilities: Visions/Premonitions
Rolfston's mother
Book: Pointed Love

Doc (Dr. T, Albert)

Species: Alicorn
Mate: Emma
Job: Doctor
*Special Abilities: Some healing, visions, magic,
    immortality*
Book: Pointed Love

Ian
Species: Vampire
Mate: Berkley
Job: Leathersmith, Blacksmith
Special Abilities: Speed
Shaye's friend
Book: Forged In Love

Berkley
Species: Fae
Mate: Ian
Job: Owner/Potter, The Winged Potter
Special Abilities: Can sense auras and species, slight healing ability, senses magic/spells
Rolf's friend
Book: Forged In Love

Gawain
Species: Falcon shifter
Mate: Merri
Job: Historian/archeologist
Rolf's friend
Book: Linked in History

Merri (Meredith)
Species: Witch
Mate: Gawain
Job: Librarian
Tess's sister
Book: Linked in History

Vlad (Vladimir)

Species: Vampire

Evil father of Rolfston

Note: Appeared in Bite Me Again. *Vlad had been attempting to gain supporters to take over the paranormal world. When Rolf wouldn't join him, he tried to kill him.*

Sheriff (Gage)

Species: Griffin

Mate: none (yet)

Job: Sheriff of Rockfort, Warden

Special Abilities: Very strong magic, tracking magic, can tell other rare paranormals

Duncan

Species: Dragon

Mate: Marge

Job: Sculptor

Special Abilities: Dragon fire

Note: Vlad killed his sister. Assisted in battle in Bite Me Again.

Book: Hoarded Secrets

Marge

Species: Cat shifter, black jaguar

Mate: Duncan

Job: Librarian in Rockfort, Guardian of the Library

Book: Hoarded Secrets

Marco

Species: Gargoyle
Job: Hunter for Wardens
Special Abilities: Tracking
Note: Warden, Gage's brother. Helps the Clan in A Hairy Situation, Forged In Love, Linked In History.

Jimmy

Species: Otter
Special Abilities: TruthSpeaker
Note: Kidnapped by Barry, helped Marge. Adopted by Marge and Duncan.
Book: Hoarded Secrets

MINOR CHARACTERS

Samantha

Species: Brownie
Note: Caretaker for Emma's farm in England, weaves, and quilts blankets. Mentioned in Pointed Love.

Douglas

Species: Gnome
Note: Ferrier, Sculptor, helps on Emma's farm. Mentioned in Pointed Love.

Thalia

Species: Unicorn
Note: Doc's mentor growing up, deceased. Mentioned in Pointed Love. *Healer.*

Jacob

Species: Human

Mate: Terrance (bear)

Note: Emma's friend, deceased. Mentioned in Pointed Love. *Nickname Hennie Pie. Emma's farmhand when she was human in England.*

Ter (Terrance)

Species: Bear shifter

Mate: Jacob

Note: Deceased. Mated to Emma's friend Jacob (mated in the afterlife). Mentioned in Pointed Love.

Charlotte

Species: Human/Vampire

Note: Ian's mom. Mentioned in Forged In Love. *Farmer.*

James

Species: Human/Vampire

Note: Ian's dad, Mentioned in Forged In Love. *Farmer, blacksmith.*

Robert

Species: Vampire

Mate: Aggie (Ian's aunt)

Special Abilities: Speed

Note: Ian's uncle in-law. Mentioned in Forged In Love. *A Lord (in England).*

Agnes (Aggie)
Species: Human/Vampire
Mate: Robert
Note: Ian's aunt. Mentioned in Forged In Love.
Artist (painter)

George
Species: Vampire
Mate: Matthew
Book: Mentioned in Forged in Love. *Note: Robert's
brother. Robert is Ian's uncle.*

Matthew
Species: Vampire
Mate: George
Book: Mentioned in Forged in Love.

Clara
Species: Vampire
Book: Mentioned in Forged In Love. *Ian's cousin.
Currently a Broadway actor.*

George
Species: Human
Book: Mentioned in A Hairy Situation, *Sam's
produce supplier.*

Graeme
Species: Human
Book: Mentioned in Forged In Love, *showed Ian
around his workshop, discussed ideas for Ian's
own forge. Blacksmith.*

Bert

Species: Human

Book: Mentioned in Forged In Love, *part of the hunter group that shot Ian.*

Carly

Species: Human

Book: Mentioned in Forged In Love, *young nosy cashier in Ian's parents' town.*

Dan

Species: Vampire

Book: Mentioned in Bite Me Again, A Hairy Situation, *Vlad minion. Attacked Sam/Tess.*

Roger

Species: Vampire

Book: Mentioned in Bite Me Again, A Hairy Situation, *Vlad minion. Attacked Sam/Tess. Delivered poisoned blood to clinic/Rolf in* Bite Me Again.

Tim

Species: Human

Book: Mentioned in Pointed Love. *Wood carver at winter market. Shelly (wife), Natalie (daughter, just had baby girl), 2 sons.*

Rob

Species: Unknown/Paranormal

Book: Mentioned in Linked In History. *Archeologist, friend of Gawain.*

Daryl

Species: Jackalope

Book: Mentioned in Linked In History. *Rob's dig was on his land.*

Barry

Species: Vampire

Book: Mentioned in Linked In History. *Convocation member.*

Randy

Species: Alligator

Book: Mentioned in Linked In History. *Archeologist.*

Rick

Species: Human

Book: Mentioned in Linked In History. *Sheriff near Yellowstone, friend of Gage. Human but has paranormals in his family.*

Rhonda

Species: Bear shifter

Book: Mentioned in Linked In History. *Shopkeeper in town.*

Angie

Species: Human

Book: Mentioned in Linked In History. *Hotel front desk.*

Steve

Species: Human
Book: Mentioned in Hoarded Secrets. *Disbelieving townsperson.*
Mate: Marshall

Marshall

Species: Tortoise, mechanic in Rockfort
Book: Mentioned in Hoarded Secrets
Mate: Steve

Paul

Species: Human
Book: Mentioned in Hoarded Secrets. *Almost hit Marshall as a turtle. Has pet rabbit.*

Gary

Species: Unknown
Book: Mentioned in Hoarded Secrets. *Lawn care, handyman.*

Dave Youger

Species: Witch
Book: Mentioned in Hoarded Secrets. *Friend of Jimmy.*

Sherri

Species: Human
Job: Receptionist at Doc's clinic

Beth

Species: Human
Mate: Josh (witch)
Job: Florist/Owner, Rockfort Blooms.

Mary
Species: Human
Mate: Bill
Job: Bakery owner

Bill
Species: Human
Mate: Mary
Job: Bakery owner

Baz
Species: Vampire
Book: Mentioned in Warded Bond. *Elliot's cousin.*

Sean
Species: Human
Job: Deputy in Rockfort
Book: Mentioned in Warded Bond

Doug
Species: Human
Job: Deputy in Rockfort
Book: Mentioned in Warded Bond

Eric
Species: Unknown (paranormal)
Job: Convocation Lab Tech, checks in evidence
Book: Mentioned in Warded Bond

Tom
Species: Unknown (paranormal)
Job: Convocation member, ally
Book: Mentioned in Warded Bond

Brandon
Species: Unknown (paranormal)
Job: Convocation member
Book: Mentioned in Warded Bond

Doris
Species: Human
Book: Mentioned in Warded Bond. *Sheriff's office receptionist.*

Ellen
Species: Vampire
Book: Mentioned in Warded Bond. *Elliot's aunt.*

Sheryl
Species: Vampire
Book: Mentioned in Warded Bond. *Elliot's mom.*

Rog
Species: Vampire
Book: Mentioned in Warded Bond. *Elliot's cousin.*

Bob
Species: Vampire
Book: Mentioned in Warded Bond. *Elliot's uncle.*

Jack
Species:
Book: Mentioned in Warded Bond. *Gage's friend, fellow Warden.*

Hector
Species: Jackalope
Book: Mentioned in Warded Bond. *Daryl's nephew, pilot.*

Leo

Species: Snake shifter
Book: Mentioned in Warded Bond. *Rick's uncle,*
*   federal agent.*

Thorn

Species: Unknown (paranormal)
Book: Mentioned in Warded Bond. *Daryl's nephew,*
*   pilot.*

Neil

Species: Phoenix
Book: Mentioned in Warded Bond. *Rick's uncle.*

ABOUT THE AUTHOR

I have loved reading since I was a child. I also enjoy baking, photography, and seeing new things. My favorite books are romances with a happily ever after. The world is a crazy place; sometimes escaping into a great book is the only way I can truly relax. Happily ever after is my favorite type of book, so my stories will end with an HEA, even if the road is a little bumpy getting there. I currently reside in the Midwest with my family.

If you sign up for my newsletter, you will get a free short story! *Christmas with the Nightwood Clan* is a glimpse into the Clan's first Christmas together and takes place during the Christmas in *A Hairy Situation*.

www.HarperDakota.com
www.Harper Dakota.com/newsletter
Harper's Readers Group

ALSO BY THE AUTHOR

The Nightwood Clan series

Bite Me Again (Nightwood Clan, 1)

A Hairy Situation (Nightwood Clan, 2)

Pointed Love (Nightwood Clan, 3)

Forged In Love (Nightwood Clan, 4)

Linked In History (Nightwood Clan, 5)

Hoarded Secrets (Nightwood Clan, 6)

Warded Bonds (Nightwood Clan, 7)

The Nightwood Clan's Favorite Recipes

Standalone

Demon's Mate